FIERCE SALVAGE

A Queer Words Anthology

Published by 404 Ink
www.404Ink.com

First published in Great Britain, 2024.

Editing: Ryan Vance and Michael Lee Richardson
Proofreading: Laura Jones-Rivera and Heather McDaid
Typesetting: Ryan Vance
Cover design: Ryan Vance
Co-founders and publishers of 404 Ink:
Heather McDaid & Laura Jones-Rivera

Print ISBN: 9781916637023
Ebook ISBN: 9781916637030

Printed and bound in Great Britain by Clays Ltd, Elcograf S.p.A.

MIX
Paper | Supporting
responsible forestry
FSC
www.fsc.org
FSC® C018072

404 Ink acknowledges and is thankful for the financial support of Creative Scotland in the publication of this title.

ALBA | CHRUTHACHAIL

LOTTERY FUNDED

FIERCE SALVAGE

A Queer Words Anthology

Edited by Ryan Vance &
Michael Lee Richardson

CONTENTS

CONTENT WARNINGS INDEX

Dealing with queer lives, many stories in Fierce Salvage feature homophobia and/or transphobia. While the warnings below flag instances that are particularly overt, readers should expect to encounter more subtle mentions throughout.

Colonialism & the Immigration System: *Femme Magic; Reclaim, Retreat, Rescue*

Drugs and Alcohol: *Dykes on a Train; One Night in Barca; Fruit Potential; Holier than Thou*

Environmental Collapse: *The Last Arctic Birds of the British Isles; Landslide*

Gendered Discrimination: *My Happiness*

Housing Crisis: *Sublet; Man for a Day*

Medical Detail/Trans Healthcare: *Intimacy; Transubstantiation: A Checklist For GRC Applications*

Police Brutality: *Holier than Thou*

Pandemic: *Intimacy; Holier than Thou*

Suicidal Ideation: *Fruit Potential*

Transphobia: *Introduction; Ooh, Stick You; Salt Lines*

INTRODUCTION

As the owners of Category Is Books, we're often asked what made us want to open a queer bookshop in Glasgow. The doors opened in September 2018. Over the years, like any good queer story, different truths have been told, things misremembered. There's a variety of answers, different combinations and collages of replies.

There wasn't a bookshop like it in Scotland. We wanted there to be one. We wanted to work together. We wanted to work on something that centred queerness. We felt isolated from other queer people. We felt detached from our queer history and culture, discovering it all much later in life, growing up under the shadow of Section 28. We watched as complacency grew post-marriage equality. We knew the rights that had been fought for were not concretely given, that they could be taken away in the blink of an eye. That progress isn't linear, and history can and will repeat itself unless we fight for it.

None of these stories are untrue, but we realised early on that we were making something that not everyone would understand. A space dedicated to only queer words and voices. To others we told about our plans, we were asked, *was there really a need for it? Isn't it all okay for gay people now? Is that not quite self absorbed, just wanting to read books about people like yourselves? Well, good luck to you anyway!*

We wanted to make something that would mean a lot to the people who knew it was needed, that it was long overdue. Whilst being welcoming to anyone walking through the doors, we haven't wasted time trying to convince the dubious or convert the confused, instead focusing on whom it is for and what those people need from the space and us.

For a brief moment, embarking on the journey towards opening the shop, we applied for a small pot of funding, but were rejected because the committee thought there wasn't enough of a demand for a queer bookshop in Glasgow. We asked if there happened to be anybody queer on the panel and were told they wouldn't release any of the committee's information. We didn't push further, but we had a sense, hard to articulate, but a familiar feeling in the body, that a room full of cis, straight people had decided what queer people want and need on their behalf.

When we finally got the keys, the shop came with a random assortment of furniture and leftover trash from previous tenants. There was a closet with the doors taken off and inside was a pile of books, a strange mix of medical textbooks, '90s gardening manuals and sun-bleached crime novels, all destined for the charity shop. But we kept the closet, sitting in the corner with its doors missing. A queer bookshop with a closet already there! It seemed too poetic not be cursed or blessed or both.

The closet, now sanded and repainted, holds our second-hand books. 100% of the money made from this section goes to queer groups and organisers. Some further afield, but others much closer to home, rotating monthly. Whatever the location, all these initiatives are focused on supporting queer people's access to what is needed. Housing. Healthcare. Education. In the last six years, over 12 new queer bookshops have opened across the UK. There are more queer books being published than ever before. We are choosing to not die wondering.

The stories in this anthology speak to these issues too. Throughout, you will encounter longing Sapphic poems; tales of dykes on trains; descriptions of dancing at queer club nights and tales of gender euphoria. There are stories about getting revenge on your landlord; the distress of accessing healthcare, queers in both the countryside and the cities; gay awakenings and vignettes of the love and care we can give to one another.

These words reflect a common theme—that we are here, and queer, living our best collective, often intertwined and gloriously messy lives—all whilst our external environment hums and thrums with increasing threat towards queer people in society.

Hate is fuelled by shame. Sometimes a group of teens will gather outside, egging each other on to come in and say something. Whoever draws the short straw gets pushed through the doorway, where they linger and pretend to look at whatever is closest, while working up the courage to say something enlightened like, 'You'se are gay.' To which we say, 'Why, yes we are, are you?' and a shop full of eyes usually turn from book pages to burn through their bravado. Dumbstruck and always outnumbered, they shuffle back out, perplexed. Our pride in who we are makes it harder to shame us. We always hope those awkward teens work it out. Come in one day to have a browse and see what takes their fancy.

But more direct hostility, transphobic and homophobic, has become more frequent since the early days of the bookshop. The endless articles filled with transphobic and ever more homophobic bile have had an effect. We noticed when there was an increase in people coming to take photos from outside to post online. Furious red faces searching for things to record and be outraged by. Looking for ways to fuck with us without having to come through the already literally open doors to have an adult conversation.

We can't control how people react to us existing proudly in the neighbourhood. But we can stick lots of gay naked butts around the signs they most like to take pictures of. We can take great joy from watching as their angry expressions become torn over whether or not to share that photo. Is it worth it to also share so many handsome, delicious gay butts?

Spitting on our door windows began during the COVID-19 pandemic. We've never seen the spitter in action, in person. They always come at night to leave their offerings for us to find in the morning. Some mornings there would be so much spit congealed to the glass that whoever it was must have entirely dehydrated themselves in the process.

We found a beautiful picture in a magazine of two very buff boys in a shower together, dripping and holding one another, and added the caption 'No more spit, Daddy, we're soaked through!' The sign saved us weeks' worth of window cleaner visits. We imagined the scene: the spitter hocking something up only to be met with a dilemma, the spit held in their cheek dribbling out and over their bottom lip as their jaw dropped. The campery of it all feels like a super power.

~

Yes, they might spit on the bookshop—but inside the queers are living fiercely and showing each other how we can live these lives.

The cute afternoon dates; friends introducing each other to Leslie Feinberg for the first time; the parents coming in to ask about how best to get their teen a binder, or a gift for coming out. The squeals of joy when someone finds a book that before only existed for them as a collection of pixels online; laughing at the niche jokes on stickers and badges with perfect strangers, sharing a deeply personal sense of humour. Do you want a '*Have you Transsexualised yourself today?*' badge, or '*Heteronormativity is the plague*'?

The meet ups; the soon-to-be hook ups; the swapping of numbers and tips for HRT, exchanging knowledge about where is safe, which doctors are kind. Where is actually wheelchair accessible; which Pride is least corrupt; the best place Southside to get late night snacks; what time does the protest start on Saturday? The friends of friends of friends reminded of how small the queer world is, and how we're all a mycology.

Tourists from literally all over the world, straight off the train looking to feel at home away from home; the weepers for whom the shop hits a particular nerve, or others whose hormones are just kicking in. Queer families getting comfy in front of the picture book section, then getting to watch them move on to the middle grade books and comics as the kids get older and taller. Queers seeking other queers for birdwatching, swimming, film nights, gardening, carpools, dance parties, music jams, knitting, grieving, free hot meals.

The privilege of getting to witness the glow that comes from people allowing themselves their transness; the painted nails, the hair left to grow out alongside the finally freshly shaved or faded and coiffured; the breathing out and levelling that comes from ceasing to pretend to others that you're anything other than yourself today; baby beard hairs and whiskery upper lips, brand new outfits tried for the first time outside the house. Seeing people transition from a distance, changing and growing over time, ourselves included. The queens and older queers quietly sharing author recommendations with someone on the cusp of coming out, and telling us about titles and histories we've never heard of.

But you don't get to revel in queer joy without supporting and holding space for queer rage.

It didn't take long after the shop opened for us to realise that it wasn't just queer books people were struggling to source. We live in a country with dwindling social services and epic waiting lists at every turn. Many of these services no longer exist or are running in limited, skeletal ways. The services that survive, we aren't able to criticise, in fear of those scraps being taken away, however unfit for purpose they are. The NHS gender identity clinic in Glasgow, at a current eight-plus year wait time, is no exception to this. We've witnessed everyone trying their hardest to plug the holes in services, attempting with very little resources to fill in the blanks for one another. New rules, regulations, reports and practices are being debated over in rooms we don't have access to, in buildings we aren't welcome in. What we need, individually and collectively, is decided on by people who have no idea what it's like to be a minority, let alone belonging to an exceptionally intersectional community in 2024. We've built rickety workarounds, passing around the same surplus crumpled £20 note, depending on who needs it most at that time for too long.

And while you can't fault the resourcefulness, our courage and determination, we deserve better.

But, amongst all of this, we are reminded of a poster that hangs in the bookshop, printed in fluorescent pink and stark black: 'An Army of Lovers Cannot Lose.' The quote, taken from a pamphlet and manifesto originally circulated by members of Queer Nation at the June 1990 New York Gay Pride Parade, feels increasingly prescient today:

Being queer is not about a right to privacy; it is about the freedom to be public, to just be who we are. It means everyday fighting oppression; homophobia, racism, misogyny, the bigotry of religious hypocrites and our own self-hatred. (We have been carefully taught to hate ourselves.) And now of course it means fighting a virus as well, and all those homo-haters who are using AIDS to wipe us off the face of the earth. Being queer means leading a different sort of life. It's not about the mainstream, profit-margins, patriotism, patriarchy or being assimilated.

In 2019, the message of the first Queer Words anthology was that we were always here. In 2024, it echoes—we are not going anywhere. The stories and poems in *Fierce Salvage* serve as a reminder that something about us, the existence of queer people, is truly infinite. They show us that there is an incredible amount of connection, of friendship, endless care, desire and fierce love for one another; even if forces in the world would prefer we didn't. That in the face of hate, violence and inequality, the struggle isn't all that remains. That despite it all, there is so much strength and magnificence in queer lives.

Niamh Ní Mhaoileoin

DYKES ON A TRAIN

*'Important: After more than a century of allowing people to book
one bed in a shared single-sex compartment, Caledonian Sleeper
are ceasing this practice when the new trains come in. Solo travellers
will then have to book a First Class single berth, you will find the
two-berth option greyed out if you are travelling alone.'*

On the last night that the Caledonian Sleeper allowed strangers
of the same sex to share compartments, an anonymous lesbian
benefactor booked out the whole northbound train and
welcomed dykes to travel for free. A moveable wake, said the
invitation—a sprig of heather attached to the white linen
card—marking the end of a 145-year era of queer possibility.

I arrived at Euston far too early, nervous, looking around
for lesbians. There had been major delays out of London that
Sunday and now, as evening turned to night, the concourse was
dense with angry heterosexuals and their tired kids. I wondered
if I had been duped somehow and, because I was very sensitive
to humiliation at that time, the thought made me sweat. Why
would they have invited me, anyway? I was a bad queer in
those days, working in finance and owning a property in West
London. I hadn't been out on the scene in years and, since
my divorce the year before, had spent every Saturday night at

a well-known Italian chain in the Westfield shopping centre, eating dinner with my mother. I felt dizzy, retreated to a bank of seats near the platform, trembling as the sweat turned clammy under my clothes. But I was determined not to break my New Year's resolution, which was not to cry publicly anywhere in Zone One. So instead I propped my feet on my bag, sank my head between my knees, and instantly fell asleep.

When I woke, the aspect of the packed station had changed, though it was barely perceptible unless you were watching out for certain flashes of luminescence. Heavy boots with jaunty laces. A slash of pink hair ranging through the crowd like a dorsal fin. Tweed waistcoats, fresh skin fades, technicolour tattoo sleeves, hundreds of rings glinting on dozens of hands. They were accumulating, gathering, like grains of sand blown in on a warm wind, changing the texture of the world. As I stood up, I caught another woman's glance and there was laughter shimmering there, the kind I always used to find in my first girlfriend's eyes, back at school, when we knew something magical that no one else did.

On board, the small compartment was heaven. Plain. Quiet. Narrow like a cattle squeeze with the whitest, tightest-pulled sheets I'd ever seen. On each of the pillows, beside another sprig of heather, lay a small roll of Love Hearts. Still nervous, I twisted mine open right away, hungry for sugar. *Dyke*, read the first. I laughed and ate it. *Butch*, read the second, and then *Rubyfruit Jungle*, *L Word*, *U Haul*. I ate them all quickly, like a child, enjoying the chalky crunch between my teeth and excited to see what the next sweet had to say for itself. Until I reached the penultimate heart, that is, which said *I Love My Lesbian Mums*. My jaw stopped then and I stared at it a long time, until the sherbet edges began to dissolve, sticky in my palm, and I dropped it in the small wastepaper basket. I felt tired again and was tempted to lie down in the top bunk, just for a little while. But then I thought of my roommate. I wouldn't want her to find me like that, staring at the ceiling like a floppy disc. So instead I ruffled my hair in the mirror and applied a spritz of my most androgynous scent. Just as I was about to open the door and leave, I unwrapped the last of my Love Hearts.

Cunt, it said. And I ate it.

As I walked to the dining car, I understood the beauty of our benefactor's plan. The train's main thoroughfare was a long corridor, dimly lit, so narrow that whenever I encountered a woman walking the other way, we had to press our backs to the walls and inch past, breath sweeping across faces and chests grazing. Every now and then, a compartment door would open to my right, offering a bright glimpse of the scene inside, of women applying lipstick, knotting ties, shuffling around one another like wrestlers in tiny rings. Though there was still an hour to go before departure, the building energy of the night seemed to weave itself around me as I walked. At the end of one carriage a brawny DJ was setting up decks. A pair of queer booksellers had transformed a compartment into a travelling shop, flags draped across the ceiling, riso prints on the walls, bunk beds piled with zines, second-hand pulp paperbacks, poetry chapbooks and political texts. They smiled and offered me a badge—*Trans Lives Are Beautiful*, it said—and as I was attaching it to my lapel, moving through the gap between two cars, I collided with someone and came to a stop. I looked up. The woman was a few years older than me, wearing a vintage Italian football shirt. Neither of us moved. Instead, our eyes settled into a long hold and we stood in silence until, not able to take it anymore, I shuddered. She smiled then, finally stepped aside.

'Maybe see you later?'

I nodded. It had been so long since anyone cruised me that I had forgotten how it felt, the hot rush of possibility, the tug deep between the hips. My wife and I had fucked the night before she left, one last act of loyalty to each other, but before that it had been more than a year.

The dining compartment was like a Hopper painting but happy: packed tables bathed in greenish light, worn upholstery, a faint smell of cooking cheese. I watched for a couple of minutes, took in laughter and flirting and the beginnings of arguments. But I didn't know how to integrate myself, remained hovering anxiously by the door until the attendant—a kindly Geordie in a *Sounds Gay, I'm In* shirt—pointed to an empty seat in a four-person booth. I slid into the gap, next to a butch woman my own age, Glasgow accent, built like a basalt pillar.

'I'm Captain,' she said. 'And this is…?'

'Hibiscus, they/them,' said the young person opposite, pink-haired with a septum piercing.

'And I'm Tangerine,' chimed the third, a woman in her sixties with CEO energy, a blonde bob and a royal blue blazer. 'She/her.'

I murmured my own name and pronouns and they nodded,

smiled and waited for me to start some kind of conversation. But my mouth had dried up, it opened and closed with a series of embarrassing clicks.

'Whisky?' asked Captain eventually, lifting a bottle from the table and pouring me a big measure. We raised our cups—'to the benefactor'—and I took a sip. It was good stuff, smoky, smelled like my grandfather, who I loved as a child but who never spoke to me again after I came out to him. The others were speculating about how we had all been chosen for the trip. It had caused some tension with Tangerine's partner, who wasn't here. Hibiscus was dating a man and hadn't known if they should even mention it to him.

'And what about you, pal?' asked Captain.

I blushed. 'Well, I suppose I am…'

'Single?' she asked and I nodded. I hated to say the word. A hardcore commitment dyke, I had campaigned for the same-sex marriage bill and proposed to my girlfriend on the night the Queen granted it royal assent. Our wedding day, as I expected, was the happiest of my life. But then it was followed by 933 of the unhappiest, which neither my wife or I acknowledged, not willing to even countenance the humiliation of a gay divorce. We pushed on, renovating the house, redoing the garden, pretending with all our hearts that we didn't hate our life together, until the day came when she couldn't pretend anymore, a week before she was due to begin IVF.

'And I realised that I'd been so busy trying to live up to this bullshit hetero ideal that I'd completely neglected my queerness, you know? I had no idea who I was any more, as a lesbian…'

I had spoken the entire monologue into my cup of whisky. But now, as I paused and drank what was left in a gulp, there was silence around the table. I coughed and looked up, in sudden agony, certain I had killed the vibe. But then Captain reached over and tousled the back of my hair.

'Sounds like we need to source you a shag then, eh?'

At eleven-thirty, as the train pulled into the night, the carriage fell briefly quiet. We all stood up and someone read a poem. Her voice was rich and distinctive and, convinced it was a celebrity, I pushed through the crowd, trying to see, accidentally jostling an older woman, who flinched but then looked at me and smiled. She was wearing a beautiful gold and black brocade jacket and she rested a hand on my arm, silently instructing me to stop a minute and listen. The poem was that one by Mary Oliver. *Don't hesitate*, it said, and the woman kept her hand on my elbow for a few moments more.

The train was like a steam room by now, people glowing pink, windows fogged and dripping, clouding out the world. But we were on our way north, the orange-stained skies of London behind us, the straight people tucked up in their beds. Soon we'd be slicing between the cities of the Midlands and clattering into the north-west of England. It's not a long journey to Glasgow, really, not long enough if your goal is to change your life forever. The volume was going up, voices lifting as drinks were refreshed, music spilling in from the next carriage. The woman in the jacket had melted away and I turned around in a tight circle, looking for her or for my friends from before. Instead, I found the woman in the vintage football shirt, a few feet away, her eyes fixed on me.

'Dance?' she mouthed and beckoned me towards her.

~

The next carriage was dark, steaming and cacophonous with feminist punk pop. The compartment doors were all open and, in every tiny space, dykes were dancing all over each other, lifting and falling like lobsters in a bucket. Next to the decks, a femme in red leather lingerie was shaking martinis in a hot water bottle and dancers crowded around her, tilting their heads back so she could pour the drink straight into their mouths. The whole space smelled of damp bodies and the woman's fingers were locked with mine as she guided me through, my heart banging and my breath short. When she finally turned to face me, I surged towards her, our hips pressed flush together by the motion of the train and the pressure of strange hands and asses and chests. We swayed to the music, her thigh slid between mine. My face was in her neck, slick with sweat, and her hands were at the waistband of my jeans, nails gripping the band of fat I hated most when I looked in the mirror but which, right then, was beating like a second heart.

We danced that way for a long time until eventually there was a pause between tracks. Around us, women cheered and eddied towards the DJ. We were flipped around in the churn, an instant of near weightlessness before my back hit the window and, for the first time, we kissed. The music started again. I opened my mouth and she slid her tongue between my teeth, her body pressed so hard into mine, mine pressed so hard against the cold glass that I wondered for a moment if we could derail the train. The DJ was hitting the pop bangers now, Katy Perry signalling the beginning of the end of the set. I reached for the back of the woman's head, pulling her away by her hair so that I could look into her face.

'Let's go somewhere quiet,' I said.

~

We tried my compartment, spilling through the door and into the darkness, forgetting that there would be someone else there. When I switched on the light, my roommate startled awake and I recognised her, the older woman who had briefly held my arm in the dining car, wearing white linen pyjamas now with her white hair spread around her on the pillow.

'Oh, I'm so sorry,' I said but she shook her head.

'Don't be.'

Her voice was warm, her smile indulgent, as though we were teenagers rather than women nearing forty. And we played the part, happily, giggling as we backed out of the compartment, making out some more just outside. Then, hands clasped, we turned and followed the corridor towards the end of the train, where it was quiet but for various shuffles and moans behind closed doors. When we hit the very back of the last carriage we sat together on the floor, backs to the wall and heads close, the juddering of the machinery vibrating through our torsos. From here, we could see a long way back up the cars and watched in silence as women drifted to their beds, in ones and twos, including Captain and Tangerine, who were laughing at something together, their arms around each other's shoulders.

'I don't know your name,' I said to the woman.

'Heron.'

She turned to look at me and we kissed again, but softly this time. I still wanted to fuck her but since there was no immediate opportunity the desire had mellowed, diffused itself through my body. I was obsessed with that feeling, after so long without it, and I never wanted to give it up again.

'Can I get your number?' I asked.

She hesitated, her awkward wince hitting me like a blast of cold air. I looked away. Outside the window, flashes of lacy snow whipped by and I watched them for a long time, until Heron reached out and rested her palm on my cheek, turning my head so that our eyes met again.

'It's just that tonight has been perfect,' she said. 'I'd like to keep it that way.'

I wasn't sure I believed her. And even if I had, what she was suggesting went against my deepest instincts, the values by which I'd always lived my life. But then I remembered how unhappy I'd been in my life and for what a long time. My eyes flooded and again I tried to look away but Heron didn't let me, kept my face between her two palms, her thumbs ranging along my cheekbones, sweeping away tears as they fell. We were a long way from Zone One, I supposed, and I buried my face in her shoulder and sobbed, allowing that small loss to stand in for all the bigger ones.

But everything passes in the end. The pain ebbed. I stopped crying, a little embarrassed, and we kissed some more, the tension building again until, in one last moment of gay abandon, she climbed into my lap and we dry humped for a little while, gasping and laughing into each other's mouths. But time was short. The train would split at Carstairs, my section continuing to Glasgow and hers to Edinburgh. We stood and wrapped our arms around each other, clinging tightly for a full minute, before she kissed my neck and turned to go. I stayed where I was, watched her walk the length of two carriages, swaying slightly like an angel, until the train wrapped around a bend and she was gone.

I walked slowly back to my own door. The snow outside the window was thick enough now that the fells glowed in the moonlight. I left the light off when I entered, not wanting to wake my friend, and climbed into the top bunk fully dressed. I didn't think I could sleep, my mind was too full, my body too vivid with feeling. But the train rocked in the dark and the woman below me breathed and I did sleep before long and dreamed of somewhere warm.

The next morning, the Glasgow platform was dotted with freezing, delicate queers. I helped my roommate off the train, and we talked about the nights we'd each had, expressing our sorrow that we hadn't spoken to one another more. She was on her way to see her daughter, who lived in Pollokshields, one of four children she'd had with the husband she lived with for 32 years before coming out in her sixties. It still astonished her, she said, that this was how her life had turned out, that she could spend the night with a few hundred lesbians and the next day with her grandchildren.

After I'd waved her off in a taxi, I stood for a while in the bitter misty rain, watching an orange truck gritting the road. The snow on the pavement had already been trampled to slush by the tight, tired steps of early-morning workers, the staggering treads of all-night drinkers and the gentle patter of queer feet. They had disappeared already, my dykes on a train, like so many grains of sand, or snowflakes, I supposed, melting into the grey of the city. I was starting to feel numb with cold. I knew I should get moving, have a hot breakfast, catch my next train. But there's so much to see, isn't there? Even in the grey early morning, even standing by a bin in the rain.

A W Earl

MOTOR SKILLS

I meant to write a sonnet about gender euphoria—
instead I learned to ride a motorbike.
As though I hadn't pinned my boyhood
on a Triumph T120, blue cylinder, exhaust
smell on cold school morning, rainbow
gloss of oil by a sole, defunct petrol pump.
As though I hadn't doodled
Harley logos on my schoolwork
dreamed clutch, brake, throttle,
kick start, hot metal, oily rags and fingers never clean,
as though I wasn't always too young, too late, too clumsy,
too much the girl for it to be okay.

All great wants hurt us more than we can bear,
some failures need to feel forgone
so that we risk nothing on the try.
The truth is we build pictures of ourselves
that have no traffic with the world, weave
stories where if we changed *this*, and *this*, and *this*
the person that we always were
would bubble fragile from our dreams.
I whispered my boy-name and thought he sounded
like the kind of guy who'd press his foot down

into the turn and *fly*, graze effortless round bends,
wheel glorious, unquestioned, and at ease.

But my god, I am so bad at this,
just like I'm five foot three
and wider than a horse, and older
than I ever thought I'd be. I've never met
a motor skill I couldn't bungle, never learned
to end my phrases on a low pitch drop and not an upward curl.
There's no great roar of power here, no leathers,
I am no devil-may-care. The instructor calls me Fred,
the bike is only 125, and I am so afraid.

But still, still, he calls me Fred, and I clutch
the handlebars like small birds, left
foot lifting from the ground, clutch
slipping out and engine, engine roar
pentameter of revs and this
this is not words, not body, not
anything I've known, all giddy
with chance, and work, and strangeness of it all.
For all my life, I've stuck to walking pace,
but here, here comes the first rush of speed.

River MacAskill

SUBLET

Marco and I met at an afters. I was locked in the upstairs bathroom at Eva's duplex flat in Pollokshields trying to access some inner peace and avoid the odd assortment of her friends who had come back after her thirtieth at the bowling club. Eva and I generally hung out one-on-one, then on nights like these I remembered that she knew everyone. Someone was knocking on the other side of the door, saying, *How long are you going to be? It's been a while.* Polite but insistent, shrill from uppers. I was sitting on the toilet fully clothed, fighting the need to melt my whole self into a puddle.

I had just broken up with my girlfriend of six months and everything felt upended. She needed space to pursue things seriously with her longer-term partner of nine months, who had a salary and owned their flat. The three of us had tried hanging out together to smooth out scheduling conflicts, but seeing her with them made me needy afterwards. She said I was *asking too much,* that I was *overbearing.* The night of Eva's party, I was two nights into mandated no-contact time with my ex. By which I mean, she'd blocked me.

I stood up from the toilet seat and sniffed. He banged on the door again. *Hello?* I opened the door and recognised him from around. Marco's face would stick with anyone, his buzzcut you want to run your hands over, his jaw like a cliff-edge. The idea of going downstairs into the party revolted me. This man, though, I liked. *Don't mind me,* he said. He stood over the toilet to pee while I inspected my face in the mirror, patting my eyebrows and 'tache back in place, and snuck looks at his reflection. *Want to come for a fag?* I said. He agreed. When we got to the back court to huddle under the bare trees, we realised neither of us had anything to smoke. We stayed outside anyway. My sadness evaporated. When I told him I thought we'd met before, he touched my waist and said, *But I'd remember you.* I pulled him towards me, closing the gap between us, and we kissed.

Despite my intense attraction to Marco, it didn't occur to me at first that we could be lovers. At the time, I conceptualised myself as a dyke experimenting with hormones. Since I'd renounced the tedious horrors of heterosexual girlhood in my teens, I had gravitated sexually only towards femmes, beside whom I became comparatively butch, sturdy, dominant. When I fancied men, it was in terms of a punch-up reverse objectification that I never followed through on. I thought maybe I wanted to inhabit their bodies, not fuck them. Of course, those two desires aren't so different.

After a year or so on T, I had been getting read more as a twink. My increased sex drive made me curious about the hook-up cultures of gay men. I felt, however, that I must be invited in, worried that I would make a faux pas if I instigated anything myself. I was horny and complacent. And Marco appeared right there in front of my nose.

A few days after Eva's party, we went for a pint and then back to mine. He talked a lot, about his art practice, his friends, and weird things that had happened to him. I watched his lips move around the words in his Yorkshire accent and was transfixed. In my room, he sat on the edge of my bed and I knelt between his knees. Wet wind blew in through the gaps in the single-glazed windows, ruffling my hair forward onto his skin. He grabbed a fistful of it and I took him in my mouth.

Our chemistry was addictive and palpable, an electric fence snapping around us when we fucked in my bed, his bathroom, the park. My fears about sex with a man dissipated when I realised my topping skills were transferable. I got high on power when he squirmed under me.

And yet, the sex bit of our relationship died out pretty quickly. One morning after he left my flat, I made the mistake of texting him something sincere about how I wanted to keep the smell of him on my sheets. To put it in writing was the problem. He didn't reply, and soon any texts I received from him became evasive and scarce. Eva tried to console me over dinner. *He does this with everyone after a few weeks. He doesn't like being vulnerable. It doesn't mean he doesn't like you, he just can't express it.* The leftover emotion from my previous break-up compounded into this one and I let myself wallow. I waited for him to get in touch, not ready to let go. I felt like I would have done anything for him to just look at me again.

I think back fondly now to this innocent season of heartbreak. Little did I know the danger we'd put each other in down the line.

Sometime in late spring I started to have problems with my at-home Reiki business. I had rented a two-bed flat for about five years, using the second box bedroom to see clients for energy work three days a week. It generated a decent income, on top of freelance dog-walking and the odd bar shift. People found me through the internet or word of mouth, mostly bereaved middle-aged women or young people who wanted to work on themselves.

The leaky hole came out of nowhere. My Reiki clients spent a lot of time on their backs in the box room, eyes to the ceiling. I was always upright, so I didn't notice a change until a client opened their eyes and asked, *Has that dark patch always been there?* While they mused about the possibility of it signifying *a spirit thing,* I made a mental note to text the landlord, knowing that I would not. I handled the landlord's fragile temper by never asking him for anything and hoping he'd forget I lived there and that he owned the property. Damp must have built up throughout the next day, until an audible drip landed right on someone's forehead. I needed a new way to supplement the rent.

You know Marco's looking for a place right now? messaged Eva, when I started to spread the word online. *If it's not too weird for you both. He needs a break from living with the party gays.* My heart lit up. To be honest with you, I had plenty of other offers. Friends of friends of cousins of exes of colleagues blew up my phone asking about the room. Everyone wanted to live in this postcode, especially people from other places, who wanted to take a break from their city's housing crises for our slightly fresher one. I didn't need a sort-of ex to move in. But then Eva said, *I'll text him and gauge his reaction so you don't have to,* and later, *He'd be totally keen to take the room. He doesn't mind a leak if it's cheap.* How could I resist? I wanted another chance to be near him. I also knew how to feign the learned amnesia of gay people, where we act like sex never happened in order to continue to coexist.

He moved in as a subletter on the premise that he'd leave for New York come October, where his friend could hook him up with some under-the-table work while he tried to kick off his career as a sculptor. He brought some of his sculptures into the flat. They overflowed out of the box room into the open plan kitchen–living room: ceramic woodland creatures in various compromising and kinky positions, strung up and wrapped around with chicken wire spray-painted black. I nodded and *hmmm*ed as he hung them along the curtain rail.

Want some dinner? said Marco, the night he moved in. It was 9pm and I'd already eaten several hours earlier, washed up and put away the dishes. *Yeah, that'd be great,* I said. *Can I help?* He grabbed his keys. *No, no, you relax, you've done enough.* He went out to the shop to get ingredients then took an hour to make pasta, refusing my sleepy offers of assistance. We sat down at the table to eat at eleven, the black glass of the tall tenement windows reflecting our ghost faces back to us.

Remember when we dated? he said, after a short lull in the conversation. I smiled into my pasta, *I couldn't forget.* He laughed, as if maybe he did just now remember. *It's very mature of you to invite me to live here,* he said, *after it fizzled out.* In my memory, it didn't fizzle out so much as get extinguished by him in one breath. Now wasn't the time for arguing, though. *We're gonna have a big summer, the two of us,* he said, clinking his tumbler of Merlot against mine. *I always liked your flat.*

For a couple months, we settled into a shaky kind of domestic bliss. I started to work out of the house, visiting clients in their homes and experimenting with guided past-life visualisations that I'd read about online. When I got home, sometimes he was there on the sofa blasting deep house. He would ask about my day and we would bitch about capitalism and everyone we both knew, then go for frantic little walks as dusk fell. Marco brought hook-ups to the flat occasionally. I put in my headphones and breathed deeply, trusting in the long game. I made him coffee when he woke up in the afternoons. *Such a good house husband,* he often said with a wink. Marco kept the middle of his floor clear except for a bucket while we negotiated with the upstairs neighbours about fixing the leak. They couldn't reach the relevant pipe from their flat, they said. We had to ask the landlord.

On a Tuesday at home, I checked my phone after hiding it from myself for an hour to do some work on my website. Standing in the hallway, my heart dropped. I rushed back into the living room where Marco lounged on the sofa. I held out my phone and watched his face fall as he read the reply from the landlord. *I cannot afford to fix these problems all the time. I will come by for a chat on Friday.* It could only mean one thing. *Fuck,* said Marco. *He's gonna kick us out.*

On Friday, I channelled my anxiety into cleaning. Marco sat sullen in his room, the silent subletter. I wished he could sit with me. I thought maybe the landlord would be less patronising towards a man. He talked to me like I was twelve. *I'm here to talk to you, human to human,* he said, legs spread wide on our sofa, stupid shiny shoes on that he didn't leave at the door. He wanted to evict me, human to human, if I pushed for any repairs. He reeled off facts about mythical things like interest rates and The Market. Said the government had no right telling him what to do with his properties, all twenty of them. I vibrated with rage. *It's not worth it for me, having you here. I need to renovate, then I will sell.* As he left, I resisted the urge to slap him on his bald head.

I know I've only been here a couple of months, but I want to fight for this place, Marco said later, as we power-walked around

25

the neighbourhood trying to stamp out our rage. *We've made a home out of this place, you and me. It's been ages since I lived with a friend I actually trusted.* When I think back now, this moment was the closest I ever felt to him. Like he showed his hand and I finally had some control in the relationship. I lapped up every word.

Marco, I'm so glad you moved in. I feel so much better with you around. I didn't realise how vulnerable I felt until I wasn't alone anymore.

Yeah, like, I might not even go to New York anymore, he shouted back at me, jaywalking as the traffic lights turned green and a taxi beeped its horn. I caught up with him on the other side. *My friend says it's not the best time to go anyway, if I want to find a decent flat. Says I should save money and wait 'til spring.* I tried to conceal my excitement. He wanted to stay with me.

We gathered legal advice from every free helpline and wrote strongly worded letters via the tenants' union and tried to bargain and ignore the landlord's calls and persuade the council to step in. We looked up his business address and gathered all the information on him we could, left fake zero-star reviews on his renovation company's online profile. We got the factor to inspect the pipes. None of it moved him. Through came the email: notice to leave. He didn't know what we were capable of, the hysteria that the tedium of life under the whims of his class could induce. We didn't know either.

The first-tier tribunal to challenge the eviction took forever. In the meantime, the leak worsened. Marco slept in my bed sometimes to escape it. We would fall asleep on separate sides of the bed and wake up touching. When the landlord started phoning me at random hours, incoherent and angry, threatening revenge on my voicemail if we won the court case, things took a turn. We noticed he often called from his business landline, even late at night. Marco got territorial. Bureaucratic revenge wasn't enough.

We went one night to his office, a small single warehouse on an industrial estate, with a copy of the eviction notice. We set it alight on the doorstep with a lighter. We rang the bell, banged at the door and ran back to our bikes like teenagers.

Twenty properties in the postcode and he didn't have a home to go to. Something to do with an impending divorce, I don't know. He didn't have any kids, just a soon-to-be-ex-wife who was on the verge of moving to Gibraltar to live with her new lover at the time. We were right, he was in there. We didn't realise he had a drinking problem, and the ringing wouldn't wake him. We didn't know how flammable the cladding of his office would be.

He was pronounced dead in the hospital in the early morning. Deadly burns and heart failure. No neighbouring buildings caught alight. The emergency services came when a taxi driver in the next street noticed the smoke. We had cycled home laughing, cars beeping at us as we took up the whole road. Passed out in my bed. In the morning we woke up, unlike the landlord.

The days that followed aren't worth recounting here. Banging at the door, questions, phone calls from the station. I don't wish that kind of horror on anyone. You've probably read about it anyway, if you weren't there in the courtroom.

I don't feel regret, as a rule. I miss Marco and my life and I wish it hadn't happened the way it did. But I know I had my reasons. We did what we could with the unequally distributed resources we had. In court, the cards fell the way they fell. My lawyer was a friend of my brother's, an upstart desperate to prove himself; Marco's was a flaky old man who could barely stay awake during proceedings. The CCTV footage showed him setting the inciting fire. I could be seen only lingering in the background. I said things to save myself that didn't work to his benefit, let's say. I got a fine and three months community service. He got three years. I wasn't going to die on the hill of non-binary identity in the courtroom, and it doesn't look so good on the justice system when they throw white women in jail.

Marco has become a kind of faggot folk hero since the incident. People want to uphold him as a symbol, someone who took escalation into their own hands, who knows the meaning of true class struggle. Sometimes in the city I see stickers on lampposts with his face on it, usually scratched up. The right-wing rags loved it, needless to say. I had to change my name. I'd never done a deed poll anyway so it was all the same paperwork I'd have had to do eventually.

I live in Ayrshire now in a housing association end-of-terrace in a pretty village. It has a garden that gets the sun when it's not obscured by the Union Jack flying high on the other side of the fence. I send letters to Marco every Friday. Sometimes I send books straight from online retailers so he doesn't know they're from me. He has my number. He never calls me. I know Eva visits him, maybe a couple of others from art school, and his mum, who's moved up from England to be closer to the prison. But they won't speak to me either. I can't always tell if I still care for him or if I want him to absolve me of this flesh-eating guilt. Maybe I just need him to acknowledge my ongoing existence, to recognise that I was there too.

Once, he did write back. Said lots of things I try my best to forget. And in the midst of all that venom, a glint, the words, *Because I loved you*. Never mind that the rest of the letter detailed all the ways I had betrayed him and how he wished he'd never taken a chance on my spare room. He loved me. Once.

Robbie MacLeòid

AIG AN OIDHCHE GHÈIDH

Cha robh Irn-Bru idir aca
ach bha condoms an-asgaidh aig a' bhàr.

A' chiad sealladh, seachad air an dorast fhalaichte,
b' e fear crùbte, na dhrathais, aig a' choatcheck,
a' stobadh dha bhaga gach criomag aodaich,
saor bho ghach rud a chùmadh air talamh e.

A-steach dhan chaibeal, solast
gorm is dearg is dealrach,
dathan sgaoilte anns a' cheò,
roinnte le bodhaigean nam fear,
an ceòl teagnò a' bualadh mar
fheis fhallasach dhealasach.

Tha cowboy ann,
na bhriogais dubh leatair, is Stetson,
gun lèine ach le sùilean gach dàrna fir air;
chunnacas cuideachd He-Man ann an leotard;
is tha fear aig a' chùl, gu cinnteach air E,
air mhire, air mhire, a' suathadh
a chom fhèin, air chall
am measg na glòire.

Ach eadar an deargad is an dorchadas tha sinn a' feitheamh,
   agus thig e, agus tha am fonn a' fàs agus a' fàs agus a' fàs
   agus
seo e:

I'm every woman!
It's all in me!

Chì mi am boillsgean:
na dlùth-phògan, na sùilean
priobach, na làmhan suathach,
na gàireachan, mo ghaol
air na gàireachan. Fairichidh mi
gach boinneag fhallais orm, meanbh-
phògan bho Dhannsa e fhèin.

Chì mi aonaran, fear na lethcheudan—
tha ceist san adhair: cà bheil a chuideachd?
Caillte dhuinn,

is chan ann sa cheò seo.
Tron ghàrradh, tha nathair G4S
dol seachad oirnn. Gun teagamh, chan eil
esan a' dannsadh, na chreutair stòlda
am measg a' chaothaich, mì-nàdarra,
a shùilean air an làir is e a' dèanamh air doras
am Fire Escape. Is cinnteach nach eil,
ach tha coltas ann gu bheil e ga ghlasadh,
a' dèanamh cinnteach, gar cumail
glaiste a-staigh. Tha mo chridhe
gam dhochainn. Tha mi a' coimhead

mun cuairt, a' sireadh nan slighean às.
Dè mu theine? No sàthadh? Club Q,
Pulse, London Pub? An deargad?
'S ann orm a tha e, an t-eagal
's gun tig fear a-steach,
is nach fhaic e mar chaipeal seo,
ach ifrinn, ifrinn a dhìth air cuideigin
airson a cliathadh, clann Dè
a dhìth air dòrainn.
Laigse
am bunait na dachaigh ùire seo:
am feum cunnart a bhith anns
gach àit' san tig sinn còmhla?
Nach bhiodh e sàbhailte
—nas sàbhailte, co-dhiù—
fuireach a-staigh a-nochd

agus gach oidhche eile, gu bràth?
אֶהְיֶה אֲשֶׁר אֶהְיֶה
Tha an teagnò gam thàladh air ais,
cunbhalach a ghluasaid. Seall. Tha lèintean meise
air na h-aingealan seo. Chan eil olc
no droch fhàileadh san adhair. Chan eil ach
ceò, màna, sannt agus gaol, agus tha mo bheul làn
phògan do rudeigin, cuideigin,

's dòcha dhomh fhèin?

'S dòcha gu bheil a h-uile duine
anns an t-seòmar seo
gam iarraidh

airson tiotan
eadar an deargad
's an dorchadas
creididh mi
ann an sin.

~

English language synopsis:
Aig an Oidhche Ghèidh—
At the Queer Club Night

A Gaelic poem about the vivid sensuality and sexuality of a queer club night in Glasgow. The setting, its sounds, rhythms, and feeling are described, in a tone of utopian hope and using religious metaphor and imagery. Here one can feel at home, in community, and desired. But the presence of a security guard is the snake in the garden, the reminder that even in this holy space, queer people aren't safe; the numerous queer folk injured and killed in similar spaces come to the narrator's mind. Even still, here is where the narrator can utter, quoting God's reply to Moses, אֶהְיֶה אֲשֶׁר אֶהְיֶה—I am that I am/will be/what I choose to become.

Ross McFarlane

EXCITEMENT OVER A JOYOUS BOY

borrow my fancy skirt
we'll watch a movie on the couch

your whisky
my tea

you dance inwardly

a polaroid
hands through hair, rocking my fishnet vest over black briefs

a
fuck you
love bite

in response i will leave piano keys
on your ass cheek
and not be sorry

i don't fuck like you
you don't cuddle like I do

sometimes I wonder if we stay up all night
just so I can kiss your 8 AM shadow

you curl into my armpit grinning

like the glint of gold from a hooped earring
i find on the floor days after you leave

Ciara Maguire

MAN FOR A DAY

When they arrived, it was unclear how long they would stay. Sofia had signed the contract without reading it and paid the deposit in cash. They struggled to find somewhere at first, watched estate agents' eyes fill up with a slow hostility as they tried to work out why two women needed a one-bedroom flat, their names moving to the end of the long list of prospective tenants. Eventually, Anna stopped going to the viewings, left her name off the lease when Sofia signed it. Still, it was the closest thing to a home they had, and they were determined to make it their own. They put art on the walls though they knew this wasn't allowed; postcards and comical newspaper headlines that Anna cut out. They wiped away the dead bugs on the bathroom windowsill and hung yellow curtains in the bedroom. They had been there three days when they found the baby. Sofia was looking through a cupboard, marking off the inventory list given to them by the estate agent. She had just ticked off the hoover when she saw it, obscured behind a mop and an ironing board, nestled sweetly in a laundry basket, eyes squeezed shut like a kitten.

Neither of them had much experience with babies, so they couldn't judge the age, but based on its size and inability to speak they guessed it was a young baby, less than one year old; solid enough to sit up and coo and pull at their hair, but too soft to walk or make legible sounds. They phoned the letting agency.

There's a baby in the flat, Sofia said. *It's not ours.* There were busy office noises on the phone; phones ringing and the estate agent typing loudly. *That's okay*, the estate agent said. *Just write it on the inventory and make sure it's there when you leave.* Sofia and Anna looked at each other, then at the baby, who was smiling in a dumb, pink way. It was theirs now, as much as anything in this flat was theirs.

Since they found the baby, they took turns being the man. When it was Anna's turn she went out to work. She moved differently on those days, felt her voice shift into a low growl, locked eyes with women on the subway. She ordered an Americano and marvelled at the deep black of it, the bitter feeling in her throat. At work the emails she received were long and apologetic; she responded with only her initial:

'*A*'

On the days where she was the man, Anna found her legs growing longer and she felt less shame about using an umbrella. She walked home in the dark, felt her weight shift lower in her hips and an ease spread over her shoulders. This was her favourite part, walking at night, the space to breathe; nothing except the cold air on her bare neck. One night as she walked, she saw a glint of orange moving in the blackness. The fox seemed to feel her presence and froze. Anna stopped too, staring at the fox, noticing its bones shifting under its skin as its breathing slowed. She narrowed her eyes, waiting it out, until it suddenly turned and bolted into the night.

When Anna arrived home, Sofia was there, being the woman. The house was warm and light flooded from every surface. Anna loved these moments. *My woman,* she would say, pulling Sofia to her with a single arm around her waist. Her arms felt so much bigger, like she could pull anything towards her and it would stay. At night they made love and it felt different, Anna silent and solid, Sofia filling the space between them with her moans.

Anna loved being the man. She loved the way her legs slackened when she sat in a chair. She loved the way other men spoke to her. She used to think that being a man was about violence, but now she saw a different way to be. She felt still, sure of herself. Even when she was gone, she could feel Sofia leaning on her. She no longer answered the phone to her mother. She did what she wanted and it was easy.

On the days where Anna was the man, Sofia waited. The waiting felt long and languorous, the space between Anna leaving and coming home stretchy and painful in a way it never was before. Of course, there was the baby to tend to. Small and fat and always needing something. It opened and closed its little fists in a way that felt so personal, so entitled, that sometimes she left it in its basket, closed the bedroom door, put on her shoes, and walked out of the house. She would walk to the end of the road and feel the shape of the weather on her back. A sharp rectangular breeze, the sun a warm almond. She could feel the baby too, through the walls separating them; both of them waiting.

Some days she walked further, to the Nisa on the corner where she would buy a slushy and drink it there in the shop.

There were an impossible number of slushy machines across one wall, all separate vibrant colours. Lemon yellow. Cherry red. Raspberry blue. Sometimes she would mix them, let lemon bleed into apple green, creating a fluorescent nightmare in the plastic cup. Occasionally she brought a slushy home and fed it to the baby drip by drip, its small mouth soggy and drooling, stained red with sugar and ice. She could only give the baby what it wanted when it was what she wanted too.

When it was Sofia's turn to be the man, everything changed. Anna stayed home, her shoulders pulling back in on themselves, her eyes less adept at holding anything. She found herself in an apron at the sink, her hands turning raw under the hot water, and she felt that this was a special kind of humiliation. It was easier when she focused on the baby; something fleshy and warm and needy. She put it in its pram and wheeled it round the park, smiling at the mothers who smiled at her, who recognised something in her that she knew wasn't true. She wanted to tell them she wasn't like them; this was only half of who she was, most of the time she was someone else, all of this was temporary. But then the baby would point at a bird, or gurgle in a hungry way, and Anna would crouch in front of the pram, let the baby hold her finger in its impossibly small hand, and she would forget everything.

When Sofia was the man, she didn't come home for hours. She went to the pub after work and only sometimes remembered to text Anna where she was. At the pub she ordered pints and split packets of crisps down the seam, spreading out the bag in the middle of the table. She became friendly with the girl behind the bar, Melanie, who had started giving her the bags of crisps on the house. There was something in the way Melanie looked at her, leaning forward too much, letting her hands linger in her hair after she pushed it behind her ear, that let Sofia know that Melanie was an option to her.

She liked this feeling of having choices, of feeling that returning home was a decision and not an obligation. She felt generous on the nights she did return, untying Anna's apron and fucking her there on the kitchen floor, the scent of fresh dough and yeast rising around them. On the nights she didn't return she felt entitled to her freedom, the night belonging to her and her alone. Sometimes she went to the casino and stayed, playing and drinking and talking with the other men until the sun rose again, her shirt sleeves stained with beer and her tie loose around her neck. Sometimes she went home with Melanie, to her feminine, single-woman flat, everything stained slightly pink with desperation. She let Melanie undo her belt and put her hand inside her boxers and when she closed her eyes, she imagined an ocean moving inside her.

One morning, Sofia arrived home late. She smelled of the night, stale cigarette smoke perforating the air around her. She moved quietly through the house. Usually she would find Anna waiting, grateful and quiet, breakfast on the table. But Anna was not in the kitchen as she usually was, and there was the absence of welcoming sounds; the radio silent, the kettle empty. Sofia climbed the stairs, noticing socks slack on the carpet. She looked into the bedroom and found the baby lying on the bed, attempting to grab its own feet and smiling. It looked small and perfect, like a stranger.

The bathroom door was ajar, and when she opened it she saw Anna at the sink, foam spilling over a razor as she pulled it across her cheek.

Anna's eyes stayed fixed on the mirror in front of her as she spoke. *You took too long. I have to go to work.*

Heat rose in Sofia's chest. *I'm not done yet. It's not your turn.*

It's only a couple of hours. Anna said. There would be no conversation.

Sofia left Anna in the bathroom and went back into the bedroom. She started to undress, peeling off her shirt and jacket, hanging her tie on the back of the wardrobe door. She could smell perfume on her skin, neither hers nor Anna's, a strange peony scent. She pulled on a soft pair of pyjamas and waited, the baby next to her on the bed, biting one toe and watching her warily.

Anna came into the room, topless and freshly shaven. Sofia watched her dress, the muscles in her back flexing as they disappeared under a large pinstripe shirt. The heat that had been sitting in Sofia's chest began to dissipate. She loved Anna like this, she couldn't help it.

My angels. Anna swooped down and planted a kiss on the baby's belly, then on Sofia's cheek.

I'll be back at six. Don't have too much fun without me. She grabbed her coat from the door and was gone.

The spring sun streamed through the windows creating a glare on the TV screen. She felt it now, the seasons changing, March really starting to get going. The baby lay on a mat in front of the TV, blinking and burping. Sofia stood at the window. A young couple were moving in across the street, into the red brick tenements that mirrored her own. She watched as the two men paused over a chest of drawers, angling their bodies forwards then back, bending and failing to lift.

The baby coughed and Sofia went to it, lifted it to her chest, placed her palm on its back. She realised how little she held the baby, how instead of a maternal feeling, its warmth next to her skin released something queasy and angular. She knew this wasn't how Anna felt. She came home often to find the two of them laid chest to chest on the sofa, their legs hanging gently in the same shape. She felt the baby shift against her, hands grasping at her hair.

She softly wrestled the baby into its pram, tucked a fleecy red blanket round its chest, put on her own coat from the night before. Outside, the men had abandoned the chest of drawers and were carrying a series of smaller items into the close; lamp, record player, half dead houseplant. Sofia ignored them, pushed the pram onwards, the sun closing in on them, a faint warmth. She pushed past the Nisa, through the park, past the mums gathered by the playground, past the train station, on and on she pushed, kept pushing, the sun rising higher and the light becoming expansive, the wind in her hair tangling it, turning it to knots, the baby turning silent and sleepy, its breathing slow, and Sofia pushing on, thinking of the time before, thinking of Anna's flexing back, thinking of the sky, thinking *what next, what next.*

The title 'Man for a Day' is taken from Diane Torr's 2012 documentary of the same name.

Len Lukowski

INTIMACY

It's always a lottery with doctors, whether they convey care or make you feel guilty for existing. I am comforted to discover, from Dr Dabrowski's warm telephone manner, she is the former. She introduces herself, telling me she's from the PrEP clinic at King's College Hospital. 'I don't know if you were expecting a call?'

'Yes,' I reply, happy to hear the voice of someone who knows anything about my life. 'But. Erm, I moved. To Glasgow. A few weeks ago. I haven't really sorted stuff with the PrEP and a GP and stuff but I've run out and I do want to keep taking it.'

'Ah yes. I did see a note somewhere about you moving to Glasgow but we weren't sure if you'd gone ahead with it.' She sounds confident which is reassuring. Nice confident. So many confident people are arseholes.

'Ah. Yeah. I did. I mean, what do you suggest doing if I want to keep taking the PrEP and stuff?'

'Well, I'm just wondering about how sexually active you are at the moment. Because obviously different people are doing different things during the pandemic, so it would be good to get an idea and then we can work out how urgently needed the PrEP is.'

She pronounces her name the anglicised way, like Charles Bukowski or Jane Krakowski. I feel a glint of recognition when I hear her say it, as if the shared nationality of our surnames means something beyond who she married or who I'm related to on my dad's side. I've never been a family person. I didn't tell my parents I was moving to Glasgow till I'd been here several weeks, the sexual health clinic knew before they did. I was freaked out they'd worry about me quitting my job and moving cities at a time like this, that I wouldn't be able to handle their worry, the amplification of my eternal sense of letting them down. Ridiculous really, I'm nearly forty, my parents have little influence over, or knowledge of, my day to day life, and moving out of one of the most expensive cities on earth, when nothing is open and you've lost count of the times you've had to move is not really such a bad idea, but you feel what you feel. I can't shake that contorted feeling whenever I picture the looks of anxiety on their faces, whenever I give them too much information about my plight. Dr Dabrowski can steadfastly hold all the things I am.

'So, let me just ask a few questions if that's OK? Just to get an idea.'

'Sure.'

'Do you have a regular partner? Or partners?'

I sink back on the fancy leather sofa of the flat I've temporarily moved into. It's a palace compared with anywhere I've previously lived, though I don't know anyone in the area and my new flatmate and I have a politely awkward relationship. He doesn't even know I'm trans. Not because I think he'd have a problem with it, more I fear being an object of curiosity for a cis, straight man. I haven't had a partner in god knows how many years. I can't deal with the conflicts, the imperfections, the exposure.

'OK, no regular partner. And how many casual sexual partners have you had in the last three months?'

'I mean, I haven't had sex with anyone since December and I stopped taking PrEP for a while but I've... been talking to a few people online since I've been here, so I think I might have sex in the next couple of weeks, maybe.'

Sometimes I get doctors who are angry at me for having needs, or those who turn cold when they discover I'm trans, but when I get someone nice, I find myself looking for parents in them, in that slither of warmth, of unworried acceptance, that moment of solid ground. I know it's a fantasy—easy to romanticise the relationship of someone you only speak to for two minutes about your medication. If they have kids of their own it's probably a different story.

'And what type of sex did you have when you last had sex?'

I'm quite tame really, no orgies, no chemsex, I don't even fuck that often, too lazy, too cognisant of how rarely the act of fucking a stranger lives up to the fantasy, the expectation. Bodies are awkward when you encounter them for the first time and you're out of tune with each other's desires, needs. I used to fuck more people because they'd just be there in front of me, at the bar or the club or wherever I found them, now they're online. I have to make a special effort to meet them or let them into my space. Since the pandemic, my social anxiety has sky-rocketed, not a great time to move to a city where I barely know anyone. It was OK in my twenties, I was drunk all the time and so was everyone else, at queer clubs in basement dives or D.I.Y. gigs, we fell into friendships that way, our inhibitions stifled, into relationships. I have heard it's now not uncommon for queers go rock climbing on their first dates.

44

I've mostly felt too overwhelmed to meet with other human beings since moving, whether for sex or a walk. The vulnerability it takes to get to know people is fucking terrifying. Especially as you age, getting to know your own flaws too well, not having the stamina to cover them or protect yourself with alcohol or whatever else.

'With a cis man. Oral and… frontal,' I stammer.

'You've probably been told this but you know that for PrEP to be effective for frontal sex,' Dr Dabrowski adopts my terminology without missing a beat, as though it's the term she's been using all her life, 'you need to have been taking it for at least seven days.'

'Yes. Yes, I did know that.'

'Just something to bear in mind.'

'Yes, I'll wait till I've been doing that.'

She starts googling clinics in Glasgow for me. I want to stop her and say I could do that. I feel bad she's doing this thing that doesn't require a medical degree or any of her advanced clinical skills, that I am draining an already impossibly overworked NHS doctor, but I also want her to stay on the phone with me forever, this uncomplicated, unstifled human contact. I already know about the clinic in Glasgow but dutifully write down the number all the same. We go through when I last had my kidney function tested, when I was last tested for chlamydia, gonorrhoea, HIV. I tell her about how my last HIV test didn't work because I couldn't get enough blood out of my finger with the finger prick device in the COVID-safe home testing kit. She tells me a lot of people have that problem. She tells me not to worry.

I can't shake this feeling of need for more of whatever is being transferred in this conversation, the care that wants nothing in return, though I know it is just a person being good at their job. I can't remember the last time anyone has asked me a question that isn't, 'So what brought you to Glasgow?' or 'What's your plan?' or 'What do you do?' Completely natural, reasonable questions that put me in a state of anxiety because I don't know what I'm doing here, other than I couldn't stay where I was. Outside, snow is coming down hard, the sky like static on an old TV. I should film it when I get off the phone, I think. Put it on Instagram. Will the snow show up?

I left London because London became like the morning after a party, when you're still gurning away in the corner of someone else's flat, though you need to go home and sleep, because you can't bear for things to end. One weekend, the first weekend of the second lockdown, having moved to another mouldy room in another flat with housemates ten years my junior, the Wi-Fi cut out and this gave me a window in which I could no longer distract myself from what I was doing. I drank a bottle of red wine in my tiny room and listened to The Spook School and Sleater-Kinney and Orville Peck and only one of those bands is from anywhere near Glasgow and have long since split up, but it wasn't that, it was that I looked up at the ceiling and became acutely aware things weren't working, hadn't been for a while, that my life was careering beyond my control. Maybe that's a me thing rather than a London thing, but something had to change.

Glasgow always held a certain appeal to me, maybe just because it's not England. I wanted to go there for University when I was eighteen. 'You will be the minority if you move to Scotland,' my father sternly warned me. A ridiculous statement, particularly as it was the year 2000, Section 28 had not even been repealed, and I was out as gay and had spent the last fourteen years being bullied relentlessly at school for gender nonconformity, did he really think being an English person in Scotland was going to be any worse?

Now I'm aware of myself as another twatty middle class former London resident, coming to Glasgow and marvelling at how cheap the rent is whilst simultaneously driving it up. I kind of expect to be resented, though in my time here people have been nothing but welcoming to me, I just can't seem to internalise it the way I can with Dr Dabrowski's phone call. There's always that feeling they'll hit some landmine characteristic of mine before too long and it'll all be lost.

The conversation with Dr Dabrowski is the first time questions have been asked to me that have alluded to my body, to my queerness, my transness, in a long time. The landscapes that exist beneath the veneer of small talk, something tender and real, intimacy beyond even the awkward fumbles with the Grindr hook ups I'm telling her about, because I don't say much to them, and what does get said in those encounters with strangers could almost be a script. I know she is essentially following a script herself, but it's one that *feels* intimate without the risk of hitting a landmine.

Fucking random dudes off apps is easy, I don't know how long it's been since someone hugged me. My skin craves it, I'm starving for warmth.

Dr Dabrowski tells me the tests I should tell the clinic I'm due for. I look out of the window at the fuzzy sky, wishing I had someone to share it with other than Instagram.

I would like to find someone as messed up as me, so it wouldn't be embarrassing, who I don't know very well and would never have to see again, so nothing could go wrong, to climb under the bed in the darkness with and pretend the world isn't there.

If only for an hour.

She asks me if there's anything else I need.

She tells me to take care.

Ely Percy

MY HAPPINESS

Growing up, I wanted to be Elvis Presley. I'd spend hours before the mirror slicking back my hair, practising my left-side snarl. Even as a toddler, I'd his lyrics down pat, was the star turn at our backyard barbecues where I entertained adults with my 'gallus' rubber legs.

My father was equally obsessed. He'd Elvis records galore; for years he'd traipse round jumble sales desperately seeking a seven-inch RPM of Presley singing 'My Happiness'—a single I later discovered had not been commercially released.

The only time I saw Dad cry was the day his hero died. It was also the only time he took his belt to me: I was five, it was my first day at primary, and some pint-sized misogynist called me a 'stupid girl'; I'd come home furious, thrown a tantrum about having to wear a pinafore.

A year later, I begged my parents to take me to the school Halloween party dressed as 'The King'. Everyone else was going as a witch or a ghoul, and it was one of those rare occasions when my mother didn't force me to conform; instead, she sat up all night making a rhinestone jumpsuit.

I won a trophy for 'best costume', and all day long I walked around saying, 'Thank you, thank you very much.' Afterwards, my father took me and my mum and sister to Cardosi's for knickerbocker glories.

On the 4th of August, 1983, Dad was the victim of a hit-and-run: he'd gone to the Bell Street ice cream shop for a family-size tub of raspberry ripple when a car came flying down Inchinnan Road. John Peel was reciting the countdown on *Top of the Pops* when police knocked on our door.

After Dad's death, I burrowed deeper into my Elvis nook: I read old copies of *Elvis Monthly*, swotted up on Graceland trivia, rented *Jailhouse Rock* on repeat; I studied every word, every diphthong on every Elvis album I could get my hands on, and I made it my mission to train myself to sing just like him. My last year of primary went by in a blur, the highlights being Dad's funeral and my part as orphan Annie in our end of term show.

At high school, I'd one friend who listened to Elvis with me, but after she moved I was labelled an oddball by popular kids who thought his music sucked. I soon learnt to keep my proclivities to myself, learnt to feign interest in groups like Wham! and Bananarama.

At seventeen, I was diagnosed with anorexia and sent to an adolescent psychiatry unit. My sister, who was three years younger, was mortified because I'd collapsed at a Wet Wet Wet concert in front of girls she knew; Lee-Anne and I had never been close, but now I was persona non grata, and she made it clear she resented giving up Saturdays with her pals to see me in the nut house. My mother visited every day except Sundays because she couldn't get a bus. She also baked cakes and tablet for all the staff and complained whenever she saw me about the terrible public transport and the burden that'd been placed on her.

Apart from seeing my psychiatrist and frisbeeing food at nurses, there wasn't much else to do. Some inpatients wrote letters to friends, but I'd nothing to say and no one to say it to. Mum delivered my guitar after I said I needed to practise for my CSYS music exam, but mostly I sat glued to my Walkman whilst staring out the window. I thought about Dad a lot, about camping trips we'd gone on, songs around the fire, him playing his harmonica. I'd countless conversations in my head where he told me he loved me, something he'd never said in real life. We talked about what I'd do once I was well—I wanted to go to drama college, but Mum was dead against it. I also confessed I was 'probably a lesbian'.

In the Spring of 1990, I auditioned via video for a Musical Theatre BA. I was still in the unit at the time, but I was getting better: I'd gained weight as well as self-esteem, had become close friends with a fellow inpatient who thought being queer was mega. I'd also realised I needed to put more distance between me and my fucked-up family if I wanted to continue to thrive. My rendition of 'That's Someone You Never Forget' earned me a scholarship at a London stage school—the only way a working-class kid like me was ever getting in. My mother went ballistic when I told her: 'You're living in cloud cuckoo land,' she snarled, 'if you think you'll ever make it as a singer.' My sister was delighted I was leaving home for good.

I was twenty-five and broke when I heard about the UK Elvis tribute competition. My girlfriend, Tracy, found a flyer in our local gay bar and insisted I try out. I refused: I'd gone to so many auditions by then, experienced so much rejection, and my confidence was shot. I told Tracy we couldn't afford the entry fee, that our rent was due, and we'd bills to pay; I said I couldn't justify spending thirty quid on something I was 'never going to win'.

I'd a more honest conversation later that night with my friend and mentor, Anna Falafel, when she questioned why I wasn't signing up. Anna was the compère at a monthly drag night and a brilliant performer in her own right; she'd taken me under her wing as a fledgling male impersonator two years previously, had christened me 'Alf Alpha Falafel' aka 'Alfie' and taught me everything she knew. Over happy-hour drinks, Anna listened as I got blitzed and reeled off various lamentations: my mother had been right all along, I was deluded, I was a loser, I was a talentless fuckwit waste-of-space who'd be better suited to cleaning toilets.

Looking back, I'm embarrassed by the things I said, especially since I knew Anna—who was a good decade and half older than me—had suffered far more disappointments in her own career. My excuse is that I was young and melodramatic, that I'd only recently realised the performing arts industry was not the meritocracy I'd believed it to be.

Anna's response was to squeeze my hand and tell me to 'keep on trucking', right before she took three tenners from her purse and pressed them into my hand. Unfortunately, my elation over Anna's incredibly kind gesture was short-lived because the powers that be decided I wasn't eligible: 'This is a contest for professional singers,' explained the note that arrived in the post alongside my crumpled application form and uncashed cheque; apparently, it was unprofessional and impossible for a 'lady' to pull off a realistic impersonation of such a masculine man.

I was so angry I couldn't speak; it reminded me of all the idiot schoolboys who'd said I couldn't do x, y or z because I wasn't one of them. It also made me think of a ridiculous story my dad once told me about how Elvis supposedly entered for his own lookalike contest and came in third.

'Fuck the patriarchy,' said Tracy. 'You should reapply as Alfie Falafel.'

So that's precisely what I did.

My lesbian pals loved the idea of me infiltrating the old boys' network whilst packing a condom full of rice. They wanted to buy tickets to watch—as did the entire House Of Falafel—but I said no. I could just imagine some drunken friend-of-a-friend tagging along and shouting 'C'mon daddy, show's your cock!' right in the middle of my set (this was standard behaviour for some of my usual audience members, and something that actually happened the very first night I performed as Alfie). No, I was adamant, Tracy and Anna were the only ones I could trust not to distract me or draw the wrong kind of attention.

Not that I expected to even get through the first heat, but I'd promised Anna I would put my entire heart and soul into it, and I was taking this promise seriously; I'd Elvis on the brain twenty-four-seven, choreographing my every movement, working on vibrato, diction, vocal phrasing. I even phoned my mother—something I rarely did—to ask for sewing tips, but she wasn't interested; her response was simply, 'Aren't you a bit old for dressing up?'

Luckily, I'd a whole month to perfect my costume, so I went to a remnant shop and bought a pattern for a pair of men's overalls, a box of silver round cup sequins and a roll of white taffeta. I was going for white-jumpsuit-wearing-covered-in-bling-seventies-Elvis, and my plan was to add aviator specs, a shaggy black side-part wig and gigantic mutton chops. I ended up having to call the cavalry (aka Anna and her drag daughters) to help with my makeup after I realised my own skills weren't up to snuff. I might've been a dab-hand with spirit gum and crepe hair, but I'd no clue how to contour and I needed folk to think I was a young man in his twenties trying to age up rather than a drag king.

As it turned out, nobody questioned my gender, and I was an instant hit with both the audience and the judges: it helped that twenty-five percent of the points were allocated based on ability to create a convincing Elvis look that captured his 'humour' and 'gregarious' personality, because I knocked that part out of the park!

Most of the other performers' outfits were on a scale of meh-to-mediocre: some had Lego hair and looked like they'd rolled around in a bargain jumpsuit basement. One guy really impressed me though, an older man with immaculately quiffed hair who turned up looking exactly like pictures I'd seen of Elvis at his 1967 wedding.

The competition got significantly harder: the Lego-hair Elvises were ousted as were the guys who looked good but couldn't sing. For the quarter finals, I wore a candy-pink blazer with oversized lapels along with a black and white polka-dot crop top, purple bell bottoms and a four-inch silver-plated star of David necklace; the judges praised my singing and my stage presence, but I nearly got booted after they unanimously agreed I was 'a bit too flamboyant'.

For the semi-finals, I wore a black jacket, black trousers, black-and-white striped T-shirt combo, and sang 'Jail House Rock' and 'Cryin In The Chapel'; I received a standing ovation for the latter.

Hearing I was through to the final was, quite frankly, a dream come true. And everything was going perfectly up until the moment I was leaving when an audience member accosted me: 'I watch you every month at the Vauxhall Tavern,' he said. 'It's great to see a young butch girl giving the boys a run for their money.'

Word spread that I was an 'imposter', and I received a suspension whilst the judges deliberated over my fate. I genuinely thought I was finished, and I was sad and frustrated because I'd worked my arse off and I knew I deserved my place. Days later, I was on my way out to the dole office when I got a phone call saying they'd decided to reinstate me on account of my 'exceptional talent'.

The night before the finals I had the weirdest dream: I awoke in a parallel universe where my dad was still alive. Parallel me was still passionate about Elvis, but because it was a passion I shared with my dad, I was able to shrug off the high school jibes; I'd a better relationship with my mother and sister, but I ended up in the adolescent psychiatry unit anyway because I was terrified to come out to them; I still applied and got into the BA, and my mum still disapproved, but my dad acted as a buffer. I went to London, became a drag king, did all the same things right up until it came to the last night of the Elvis competition when I sang 'Amazing Grace' followed by 'My Happiness'. Just as the curtain was going down for the final time, I saw Dad in the audience, and I woke up writhing and sweating.

That morning, I phoned round all my friends, apologised for excluding them. I explained that I'd been worried I'd embarrass myself, that I didn't want to let anyone down; I also said they were my family and I loved them, and I asked if they could please come to that night's show because I needed their support.

My friends turned up en masse. All apart from Anna. She made a brief appearance at the flat to say 'break a leg', and to tell me she was sorry she couldn't be there because she'd an appointment in Glasgow. She didn't tell me the appointment was a part in *Taggart* playing a cross-dressing night club singer, and I'd no idea this would be the last time I'd see her in the flesh, or that our careers were about to veer off in radically different directions.

Most of what happened next is hazy. The first half of the show went by in a flash; I remember Ray, the older man with impeccable dress sense, telling me I was doing great and wishing me luck for my final number; then I was onstage rambling into the microphone about how I was grateful to be there, how I wanted to dedicate the performance to my dead dad; then the piano was playing and I was singing for dear life.

I remember all the Elvises gathered onstage as we waited for the verdict, how my knees felt like they were buckling when they read my name out as winner of the gospel category. Then they announced I'd won the entire competition, and I thought I might vomit.

There were cheers and wolf whistles, shouts for an encore, and blood boomed in my ears as I held my hand out for the mic.

Right then, I was the happiest I'd ever been in my entire life.

Shane Strachan

BASTART BAIRN

Sweet Willy's taen him o'er the fame,
He's woo'd a wife and brought her hame;
He's woo'd her for her yallow hair,
But's mither wrought her meickle care;
And meickle dollour gar'd her dree
For lighter she can never be;
But in her bow'r she sits wi pain
An' Willy mourns o'er her in vain.
          —from 'Sweet Willy', traditional ballad

25/12/1992

A screen o black-and-white fuzz and a faint hissin soond…
And then a blur o colour and these bairnies' vyces—yours
and yer sisters—high pitched and loud. The picture gings
clear and ye can see baith o yer dark blonde heids. Four
years aul, ye hop aboot the livin room in yer Rupert the
Bear pyjamas, a reid tap and wee yalla troosers, surroondit bi
presents on Christmas mornin. Ye scance the room, searchin
for the one present ye'r really aifter, that ye'v been lang sikin.

Yer sister is five gan on six. She starts rippin intil her
presents doon on the grey carpet, and ye'r quick tae tak een
aff yer ain pile on the black velvet cooch. Ye start haulin aff
the paper—it reeshles in yer hands afore faain doon ontae

the fleer. In the backgroon on the TV, a Christmas cartoon plays. *What fun it is to laugh and sing a sleighing song tonight…*

Look fit I got! A scootie gun! ye say, huddin up the neon-green Super Soaker tae the camera—it's near the heicht o ye. Ye turn roon tae yer sister. Look Charlene! Look fit I got.

Hey! Ye'r nae squirtin me.

Aye, but I just gotten it. Look.

She disna show ony interest so ye turn back tae the camera and haud it up.

I love this. I jist love this—

It's nae clear if ye then say *gunnie* or *duddy*—nae clear if ye've aaready been telt tae caa the man ahin the camera *dad* yet, or still jist Zander.

Ye better wyte till yer mam comes doon, he orders. Ye baith freeze on the spot, presents half opent in yer hands.

Mither! yer sister shouts. Hurry up! We're nae openin mair presents until ye come doon.

Yer mam appears at the door and maks her wye through the room, closer and closer tae the camera. Her feet are bare aneath her black leggings. She's on a baggy grey T-shirt that canna quite hide awa her widenin hips and swallt belly. Her dark hair is permed in ticht curls, and her tired green eyes avoid the camera as she snakes through the presents wi a packet o Regal Kingsize, a lichter and a glass ashtray clutched in her hands. She keeps sniffin as though she has a caul or she's just been greetin.

Look fit I got, mam! ye say.

Ooh, she says tryin tae soond enthusiastic afore sniffin again.

Yer sister unwraps mair o her Santa presents as fast as she can—a Minnie Mouse backpack, a dressin goon, a mug, a hairband…

Erasure tape! She shrieks wi delicht, haudin up a VHS with a purple cover that says ABBA in big letters. She rushes ower tae the TV and puts in the tape. The Christmas music stops and Erasure's version o 'Lay All Your Love on Me' begins.

Ye get through yer presents at a slower rate: toy cars, a Hulk Hogan action figure, anither gun, a dressin goon, a set o magic tricks, a Magna Doodle...

He's got mair than me! Charlene huffs.

Aye, but you've got a big een, mam says. Yer washin machine! You wis jist wuntin a washin machine and Santa's geen ye a tumble drier and an ironin board an-aa. You'll hae tae dee aa the washin noo!

But it's nae workin, Charlene says afore smirtlin tae the camera. I'll hae tae get a plumber.

Yer mam moves awa fae ye and sits doon next tae yer stepdad as he keeps filmin. In the corner o the screen, her fag appears noo and then, the tip o ash gradually gettin langer. Charlene coughs and splutters as she unwraps anither present tae reveal two ootfits for a Cinderella dall that there's nae been ony signs o yet. Ye look roon at yer ain Santa present pile and check in case ye've missed ony—in case maybe the dall is in your pile—but they're aa unwrapped.

Earlier in the year, fan yer mam had nae lang left yer dad, ye were walkin roon Woolies wi her. She wis weerin yalla boots and a hairnet, reekin o fish fae her new guttin jobbie. Ye spied a dall in Woolies ye wanted. Nae Barbie or Sindy, but some ither thing that wis only a couple o poond wi yalla hair and an orange and pink frock. The dall wis sheathed in a plastic case glued tae a bit o cardboard, raither than in a proper box. Ye asked yer mam for it. She said No straight awa. Ye asked again. No again, but louder. Ye started baalin greetin in the middle o the aisle, ower thrawn tae move. Eventually yer mam snatched the dall oot yer hand and went and boucht it tae ye. Yer sister laughed aa the wye back tae yer nan and dyde's. Then they laughed an-aa fan they saa ye come intae the lobby clutchin the dall.

But that's fir quines! they roared.

Wi yer heid doon, ye marched upstairs oot o sicht. In the lavvie, ye taen a pair o toenail sheers oot the cupboard and ye cut the dall's hair aff, lettin the strands o yalla plastic faa doon intae the toilet bowl until she wis almost completely baldie. The dall looked mair like a loon noo, but that didna tak awa the heavy feelin in yer belly. So ye chucked her intae the lavvie as weel, and ye flushed, and flushed, and flushed, but the dall's legs widna disappear roon the U-bend. Aathing felt stuck and knotted up inside yer belly. Ye lay doon in the spare bedroom and grut intae the pilla until the feelin faded awa.

Noo the Santa presents are deen, ye mak yer wye across the rest o the room, openin the presents fae faimly. The first is fae een o Zander's brithers. It's a big Troll wi green hair and a white hat tapped aff wi a fluffy reid pom-pom. Ye scream wi excitement.

I'm gettin spiylt wi this Trolls!

Yer mam and Zander laugh.

I'm gan tae sleep wi him the night, ye say.

Ye'r gan tae sleep wi him the night? Aye, aye! Zander says afore shakkin his heid. In the backgroon, Erasure sing 'Take a Chance on Me' on the TV. They're dressed as Agnetha and Frida, weerin thick blue eyeshada and pink lipstick.

The hame video suddenly jumps aheid. Yer mam is noo ahin the camera and Zander is on screen. Caught up on sleep aifter his maist recent trip at sea, he flits aroon the room finding presents tae pass tae ye. He's weerin faded blue jeans and a white T-shirt that has cartoon figures on it, lyin doon on sun loungers by a beach. Fan he gets near enough the camera, the words CLUB 18–30, IBIZA are visible. Pokin oot fae his left airm sleeve is his latest tattoo—a mermaid sat on a rock, her tail curvin tae one side. Yer mam's name is in black letters aneath it in a handwritten style. The Christmas music is back on the TV. *The horse was lean and lank. Misfortune seemed his lot...*

Right! Fae Alma and Sandy! Zander says as he hands ye the gift fae his mam and dad.

Eurgh! Sellotape. Sticky hands, ye say as ye flick the Sellotape ontae the fleer and then rip aff the paper. Ye reveal a box that reads WHACK ATTACK in big yalla letters above two bairnies wi blonde heids, jist like you and Charlene. The loon has a yalla hammer in his hand, his moo hingin open as he thumps a wee pink mannie's heid intae a green disk.

Wow, I hivna seen that game afore, yer mam says.

Ye open up the box and tip the wee disks oot ontae the fleer. Ye dinna bother tae unwrap the hammer fae the cellophane afore using it tae whack doon the wee mannies' heids. Yer sister opens mair presents ahin ye.

From Alma and Sandy, she reads. She unwraps a selection box. I'm fed up o sweeties! I'm gan tae be fat!

Ye'll maybe be as fat as me! yer mam says.

Oooh! I'll hae tae diet, Charlene says tae the camera, pattin her belly as you keep hammerin awa at the loud, tickin disks.

She unwraps anither present fae Alma and Sandy—a baby dall.

You've an affa lotta babies! yer mam says till her. Ye'll have tae get in practice though, eh?

Charlene giggles. Ye whack harder wi the plastic hammer, ignorin Zander as he shouts for ye tae come open mair presents.

Whack. Whack. Whack.

Three months afore, Zander had picked ye aa up in his boxy reid car fae yer nan and dyde's hoose, far ye'd been biding ever since yer mam left yer dad. Ye drove under grey skies oot alang the edge o the toon, past the sand-coated ceemetry bi the beach, and then on past the golf club for anither couple o mile until ye came tae Cairnbulg, the village far Zander had been broucht up. His mam and dad's hoose wis on a street corner—a gairden filled wi chuckies and an owergrown bush bi the front door. The wheels o the car crunched across the chuckies in the drive. Alma and Sandy's wee bichon frisé, Honey, jumped up and startit scratchin at the living room windae. She barked as ye walked past tae the front door as though ye were intruders.

Alma wis wytin at the lobby wi a lit fag in her hand. Even wi a thick wooly jumper on, there wis naething o her compared tae yer nan and grandma. Her wee legs bucklet like a frog's in the dark leggins she had on.

Fit like aabody? she croaked. Come awa ben.

Ye aa followed her through intae the living room, yer mam haudin her hands in front o her belly. Like Honey's fur, the waas o the living room were yalla wi the fag smoke that made the air hazy and stung yer een. Sandy wis in his airmcheer, takkin deep draas o his ain fag, his eyes fixed on the TV. He finally looked up at you and Charlene and seemed surprised tae see yis, as though he'd nae idea that the dog had been barkin and that Alma had ever left the room.

Across fae him, his two ither loons sat on the fleer. The youngest had on a basebaa cap, but ye could see his pupils were wide and dark aneath, like he wis under some kinda spell. The aulest brither's heid wis bald fae the treatment he'd been gettin at the hospital for being nae weel. Ye'd been waarnt fae yer mam nae tae ask aboot his baldie heid in the mornin. Baith o the brithers were puffin awa on fags an-aa. Yer throat tickled and ye sair needit tae cough, but ye were too feart tae attract ony attention tae yersel so kept swallaein the tickle awa.

In silence, ye sat doon on a sheepskin rug in front of the electric fire. Cups o tae and coffee were soon passed roon the grown-ups afore tumblers filled wi orange diluting juice were handed tae you and yer sister, dark in colour and ower sweet tae the taste.

Fit a fine it is tae hae aa my loons and Sandy hame fae sea at the same time! Alma said as she took her seat. Aabody smiled in agreement, and then anither wee silence.

So, we've some news for ye, yer mam said, her een constantly blinkin.

Oh? Alma said afore onybody else could tak a breath. Her lips made a wee circle, draain aa the deep lines roon her moo towards it.

Go on Charlene, you can tell them.

Yer sister sat up and faced Alma, as though she wis aboot tae perform a poyem.

Mam's haeing a baby! she scraiched.

Ye'r pullin oor leg?! Alma looked up at Zander.

We're nae. She's three months aaready, he said afore snicherin.

Sandy and his ither loons sat staring at Alma, wytin for her tae say summin mair.

A grandchild! Fit a rare! Alma said, her throat catchin as though she micht greet. Oh! I mean… Anither grandchild. She leant ower and rubbed the tap o yer heid wi her yalla fingers, then flashed her yalla falsers at Charlene fa wis oot o reach.

That's grand news, Sandy said.

Aye, said Zander's brithers in unison.

It went quiet again for a mintie. Ye took a sup o yer juice as the electric fire tinkled behind ye. Yer back felt ower warm and it wis startin tae mak ye feel sleepy alang wi the constant haze of fag rik.

So, dae ye ken fit ye'r gettin? Alma asked, rubbin her hands thegither. Fag ash snowed doon across her lap.

No, nae yet, yer mam said. It's too early tae tell.

Ye looked ower at yer mam's belly and thought o the baby hiding inside and wondered yersel fit it might be.

Oh! Imagine if it is anither loon in the faimly. Alma said. Her een turned glaissy at the thoucht, but then her smile drapt and her face stiffened. And fan ye gettin mairriet? she asked.

Yer mam looked roon at Zander, her een widenin.

We're nae gettin mairried, mam.

Fit? Alma lowpit up in her cheer. Her back straightened apart fae the wee curve she ay had in her neck. Nae grandbairnie o mine'll be a bastart!

Zander's youngest brither snort-laughed intae his hand. The ither brither ended up deeing the same.

Fuck's sake, mam! Dinna sweer in front o the bairns! Zander said.

Oh, sorry! Sorry…

Yer mam's een kept dartin atween Zander and the fleer.

My divorce'll tik a filie yet, and I dinna think I can pit masel through aa that weddin palava again, she said quickly. She tried tae smile, but her moo ended up quiverin shut.

Alma looked roon at Sandy, but he wis busy lightin up anither fag as though naebody else wis in the room.

Weel, ye'll hae tae get that divorce sorted quick then, Alma croaked. Ye'll be mairried afore that bairnie's born. Mark my words.

Come on Shane! We've nae got aa day. Come and open up mair look! Zander is shoutin at ye. Ye finally pit doon the Whack Attack hammer and mak yer wye ower tae Zander fa hands ye a parcel. Ye unwrap it tae reveal two fluffy pink dog slippers. Yer face lichts up wi a smile.

I think they've mixed up, Zander says as he wheechs the slippers oot yer hands. Angela's mixed up. Ye'r nae gettin the pink eens. No way! No, no, no, no.

I'll tik them! Charlene says, runnin across the living room wi a different pair o dog slippers in her hands. You can tik this broon eens.

Zander helps ye pit them on yer feet.

That's mair like it now, is it? yer mam says fae ahin the camera.

Ye canna be a handbag aa yer life, eh? Zander says, nudgin at yer shooder.

Woah! Charlene shouts, haudin a purple box up tae the camera. It's a Cinderella dall dressed in a blue satin goon. Thank you mam and Zander!

She runs ower and gies Zander a kiss on the chik, then runs doon ahin the camera tae dee the same tae yer mam.

Zander hands ye a present o a similar shape and size tae open. Yer een widen.

This een's fae yer mam and me, look.

Ye gently unwrap the paper, careful nae tae damage fit ye think is inside.

I hope it's a...

Ye cut yerself aff fan ye recognise the word *Cinderella* on the tap o the box. Ye start screamin and jumpin up and doon—the maist noise ye've made aa mornin. Ye unwrap the rest o the paper tae reveal a Prince Charming figure dressed in reid briks and a white jacket trimmed wi gold. He hauds a smaa blue pilla wi the glaiss slipper stuck ontil it.

Oh, that's you happy noo, look, Zander says. Noo ye've got a Prince!

Ye turn the box roon in yer hands and point tae the picter o Cinderella on the back.

And ye get the bride in this een, ye say, lookin hopeful. Ye quickly turn the box roon and press it close up tae yer face, searchin for the bride Cinderella inside—maybe ahin Prince Charming? But she's nae there.

Ye open the box and tak Prince Charming intil yer hands and inspect the black hair painted ontae his wee plastic heid—ye mind hoo the smell o the pine tree in the corner o the living room wis owertaen by the scent o fresh plastic, sweet and sickly.

Fit wye is Shane's rubbish ower aside mine? Charlene shouts. I'm gan tae kill Shane. Aa this rubbish!

Fit an affa stuff here Shane, Zander says. It'll be like flittin aa the weddin presents again, win't it?

Ye dinna tak ony notice o Charlene or Zander. Ye come up tae the camera tae show yer mam Prince Charming up close. She reaches oot wi her left hand and taks the toy fae ye. The wee diamond in her new ring glisters in the licht—the ring ye watched Zander pit on her finger at their weddin just three wiks afore. She hauds Prince Charming up tae the camera and he fills the hale screen. He's the same length as the baby boy growin inside her belly, the baby nae lang saved fae being a bastart bairn.

Etzali Hernández

FEMME MAGIC

the me that existed
   before the immigration
       system   t o r e
           m   e
       a p a r t
is long gone.

the me that rose from
it is standing here
powerful like my ancestors' presence.

truths have broken up my world
into
f   r   a   g   m   e   n   t   s
                                              w i t h
                                            h   a
                                            r   s
                                            h
                                                e
                                          d
                                                g
                                          e
                                                s

i exist in a different world
wearing [battle] scars,

scars,
speaking out for myself every moment,
fighting for what matters to me.

effort became magic

my mind resounds with love and freedom
alike i give my community credit
for the place i am now.

after years of struggling,
several things became possible, indeed.

somedays, i'm waking up from restless nights with glorious
    dreams:

        i'm a fierce femme smashing the patriarchy,
            defying your white hetero normality.

this   l i f e of mine
          is an intricate,
               beautiful,
            powerful
               brown oddity.

Rhys Pearce

TRANSUBSTANTIATION: A CHECKLIST FOR GRC APPLICATIONS
For Hilary Dawn Cass OBE

My wish to wear a dress is the subject of at least two medical papers. Check

A day in my life is the stuff of conspiracy theory. Check

My sexuality is a weapon of mass destruction, and should be handled as such. Check

During orgasm, my nipples become the nails used to execute Christ, but retain their standard appearance. Check

Around the age of six, I was replaced by an identical child who will one day catalyse the apocalypse. Check

The act of shaving my legs crashes economies and topples governments. Check

I single-handedly killed the tie industry. Check

I then proceeded to devour the corpse of the tie industry to eliminate all evidence. Check

The death of my present incarnation will only reveal a stronger and more questionably dressed form. Check

The fact of my access to the internet causes one nervous breakdown every thirteen minutes. Check

I am impervious to all weapons except lamppost stickers. Check

I must be filtered out from the water supply to avoid
    ecological catastrophe. Check
I am wolf-whistleable from a distance of at least one furlong.
    Check
My name must not be uttered at all costs. Check
I am often known to manifest as a grimy substance in women's
    bathrooms. Check
I am only visible when wearing the skin of my prey. Check
I am responsible for a general trend towards moral degeneracy.
    Check
I am responsible for unemployment and shrinkflation. Check
I am responsible for my own safety. Check
I am responsible for my own persecution. Check
I am failing to live up to your expectations. Check
My health is an act of malice. Check
My skin cannot be penetrated by love. Check
I am an opening band of a woman. Check
My heart beats at a frequency that constitutes political
    extremism. Check
My pulse violates BBC-style impartiality rules. Check
My suppression justifies the use of supra-judicial emergency
    powers. Check
My life is as valuable as single-ply toilet paper. Check
My existence must be kept secret from the vulnerable. Check
My every waking moment is to be measured on a weighted
    scoring system against contradictory metrics. Check
My vocative pronoun is 'saboteur'. Check
I come with a 'panic' button set into my forehead. Check
I should be targeted with nuclear weapons. Check
I deserve no places of shelter and can be afforded no mercy.
    Check

I have been convicted of identity theft against the being
   formally known as myself. Check
I was industrially synthesised in a German lab in 1943. Check
I am in violation of community guidelines. Check
I am the cause of the bronze age collapse. Check
I am the cause of road closures. Check
I am in this for the money. Check
I have purpose-built my gender to be as unrecognisable as
   possible. Check
I inexplicably self-destruct. Check
I do not deserve this Check
Gender Recognition Certificate.

Carrie Marshall

OOH, STICK YOU

Every day, my dog and I go for a walk. We're new in town and we've found a nice place just round the corner from where we now live, a small but leafy park where we can escape for a while from the many unopened boxes that fill every floor. My dog likes the park a lot more than I do. That's partly because she's a dog and I'm not, but it's mainly because my dog can't read. That means she can't see what the shiny vinyl stickers on all of the bins say.

The stickers are, of course, transphobic.

These aren't home-made like the ones by the 5G fantasists, the football fans or the fascists. They are professionally made and machine guillotined, not inkjet printed and scissor cut. They are unattractive, uninspired and unoriginal. Some have the familiar black and white branding of the Nazi-adjacent grifter who's been coining it in for years from the quick to click and slow to think. Most are brightly coloured, sporting the kind of fonts and emoji normally only found in Facebook threads. Some try to be funny, although their creators only know the one joke. And a few are literal false flags, pride or trans pride flags behind inflammatory statements designed to make it seem that we're the extremists.

The stickerer, I'm certain, is local, lazy and lucky. Local and lazy because her—and you can be sure she's always, emphatically, a her—stickers only appear here, in this small area; if I chose to walk my dog slightly further afield I wouldn't see a single one. And lucky because her home and her stomping ground are right in front of the high school, enabling her to target the teens who wander and gather here every weekday, teens who will no doubt include trans and non-binary kids, without the slightest bit of effort or inconvenience on her part. A quick walk and she's home and warm again, ready to bask in the approval of her online enablers, earning another social media medal for her bravery in remotely bullying a couple of bairns.

They say that with religious and political conservatives, everything is projection: what they accuse others of doing is what they themselves love to do or dream of doing. I think that's particularly true here, because our stickerer is getting off on this.

In another world, the stickerer would be a flasher, an indecent exposer. Because for them to have their fun, there needs to be a victim. A dick displayed or described to nobody is a dick that isn't going to deliver the dopamine.

The thrill here isn't in the doing. It's in the doing it to somebody else. The upset, the alarm, the cruelty towards people who can't hurt you back. It's so wonderfully, deliciously, delightfully *naughty*, and so much safer than shoplifting. Get caught slipping lipstick into your handbag in Boots and it's social death. Get caught doing this and you can start a crowdfunder that'll keep you in lippy for life.

Posting bought-in bigotry ordered online after the Sainsbury's shop is the most middle-class kind of crime, and I deal with it in the most middle-class way: I tut, I lift, I scrunch and I bin. I am a one-woman clean-up crew, but I am also the Sisyphus of stickers because I know that tomorrow there will be more of transphobia's greatest hits, more choice cuts from *Now That's What I Call Dogwhistles*. And when I see yet another batch freshly stuck to spoil yet another queer kid's day I'll briefly wish that their one joke were true and that I really could be an attack helicopter.

The stickerer feels safe, and she shouldn't.

I don't mean she should feel unsafe in the context of physical violence, even though that's what she wishes on us, what her far-right fellow travellers want to enact and what terrorism her movement foments from behind plausible deniability. Today's news reports include two separate stories about trans teens in bathrooms, kids the same age as the ones our stickerer targets. One, a trans boy, was beaten bloody; the other, a trans girl, had her jaw shattered and a tooth smashed. Both kids were using the bathrooms the bigots demand trans teens use, not the correct ones that should be slightly safer, but of course we know that it was never about the bathrooms.

Our stickerer has no reason to fear that kind of violence; she, not the children she targets, is the dangerous one here. And she has no reason to fear social or professional should she be caught in the act. While other kinds of bigotry still come with consequences, this particularly middle-class malaise isn't just tolerated. It's celebrated.

How did we get here?

The short answer is that there is no short answer. If this were a crime drama it wouldn't be *Murder, She Wrote*, because I am no Jessica Fletcher and the villain isn't just one jobbing actor. This is an entire Cluedo of culprits, with all the characters in all of the rooms wielding all of the weapons.

In no particular order: it was the internet and private equity destroying newspapers, their editors embracing clickbait as a survival strategy. It was producers more focused on entertaining than informing. It was social media mining revenues from rage. It was the revenge of a former first minister and his inner circle. It was dark money from Russian oligarchs and American evangelicals, their identities conveniently concealed by crowdfunders. It was contrarians making big money from bad opinions. It was Trump in the US and the far-right Tory takeover here. It was billionaires bullying their critics and then SLAPPing them into silence. It was grifters and groupthink and secret WhatsApp groups coordinating cruelty. It was a national broadcaster turned propaganda pusher, packed with political placemen and terrified of the tabloids. It was pundits and private schooled populists and phone-ins and foam-flecked old men turning TV screens gammon. It was washed-up celebrities berating a public that wasn't sufficiently sycophantic. It was authors building brands on the back of bigotry, sanitising their socials just before the book launch. It was COVID conspiracism, people losing their minds online behind quarantine-closed doors. It was a dead cat hurled by a government desperate to distract from the memory of politicians partying while the bodies piled high.

It was all of these things and one more thing, which I think might be one of the saddest: it was us kidding ourselves on.

When Scotland was judged the best place in Europe for LGBTQ+ people to live, to work and to love in the mid-2010s, we saw it as a sign of how far we'd come. We didn't see it for what it really was: a sign of how far we were about to fall.

I don't think it's a coincidence that Scotland's LGBTQ+ friendliness peaked at the same time that we were in the final stages of the independence campaign. During that campaign it felt like things were changing fast for the better. The promise of a new Scotland had transformed our politics with a much-needed injection of youthful energy and the country was on top of a thrilling wave of excitement and optimism and inclusivity that really felt like the beginning of something beautiful; we would look forward, not back; outward, not inward.

Of course we still had our pals with the bowler hats and funny walks tooting and fluting on Saturday mornings, and there were still a few Reverend I.M. Jollys who wanted to chain up the swings on Sundays. But we were going to leave all of that alongside Tennents Lager Lovelies, original Irn-Bru and Scotland's heavy industry in the past, a place that only lives on in memories and in poorly written Glasgow Live listicles.

We were all Jock Tamson's bairns, all marching under the same banner, one big happy family.

I have felt the same shock exactly three times in the last ten years: when the indyref result was announced, when Donald Trump was elected President, and when the Brexit votes were counted. Each time, the same four-word feeling like four jabs to the chest: What. The. Actual. Fuck.

I was blindsided every time, but the first time, the referendum result, was the worst time because it really shook my faith in my fellow Scots. When the victors took to George Square to celebrate with flags and flares and fists on the night of the result I stared at them in absolute horror: are they *us*?

I genuinely hadn't imagined a No victory because I *couldn't* imagine a No victory. We Scots were too kind and too clever to succumb to the politics of fear, to fall for the scaremongering of right-wing newspapers, to be conned by such pathetically obvious propaganda. But of course we weren't, and I now understand that if anything, Better Together probably put too much effort into it. They could have just called the Yes movement 'groomers' and knocked off early with the referendum result in the bag.

Looking back, it's very clear that the Scotland I thought we were living in wasn't the Scotland we were actually living in: this is, after all, a country where the most rabid right-wing rag outsells all the left-leaning papers combined by a massive margin. And with hindsight I think I ignored what turned out to be some pretty significant foreshadowing.

Towards the end of the referendum campaign, I knew that a few of my fellow Yessers were spending so much time on social media that they were beginning to distance themselves from the reality-based community. Their comments and their conversations became studded with stories of sinister forces and false flags, of too-convenient coincidences and of quislings and of shadowy figures pulling strings.

That went into overdrive after the result. Like me, they were faced with a verdict that they hadn't imagined possible. But unlike me they decided that it wasn't because the campaign had failed, that others simply weren't convinced, that the bubble we'd been in wasn't as representative as we thought. No. The No vote was a conspiracy, a cover-up. And down the internet rabbit hole they went, looking for someone or some group to blame, something all kinds of bad actors were only too happy to help them with.

I'd been in the same bubble. In our bubble we anticipated the delicious moment when we'd all vote Yes and drive the Tories out of Scotland as St Patrick did Ireland's snakes. What we didn't do was remember that while many Scots might not be able to bring themselves to actually vote for the Tories, they're often quite happy with even some of the Tories' most regressive policies.

One of the best examples of that was in 2000, when a quarter of Scotland's adult population voted to keep one of the most hated and hateful laws passed by Margaret Thatcher's government. That law was Section 28, aka Clause 2A, the law that banned discussion of LGBTQ+ lives from schools, LGBTQ+ art from public spaces and LGBTQ+ books from libraries in order to perpetuate queer secrecy and shame.

The Keep the Clause campaign pretended to be a grass-roots movement and pushed the lie that Scotland's kids were in danger from schoolteachers, librarians and what front pages screamed were GAY SEX LESSONS, defaming gay and lesbian people as dangerous, predatory deviants.

The campaign was bankrolled by one of Scotland's richest residents, who of course claimed not to be bigoted, and it was conducted primarily through despicable billboards, baseless newspaper scaremongering and via the BBC, which helpfully explained to the nation that Section 28 prevented local authorities 'from promoting homosexuality as a pretend family relationship'.

The campaign mobilised over 1 million Scots to post votes demanding that Section 28 stay on the statute books. Luckily for Scotland it was a kiddy-on referendum with no legal standing, so those votes carried no weight. But still. Just twenty-four years ago, one million, ninety-four thousand, four hundred and forty Scots chose hate.

Some of the Keep The Clause voters, I'm sure, learned to love us in the years afterwards: increased queer visibility in the culture and in people's everyday lives will have helped many people move from ignorance to understanding and even celebration. But I suspect that for many more, it wasn't that they stopped having bigoted views. They just understood that it was no longer okay to say them out loud unless you were very sure of your audience.

Bigots always predict a time that'll come when they'll be validated and vindicated, when their beliefs will no longer be considered unspeakable. But I wonder if even the most deluded members of the Keep The Clause crowd ever dreamed that when they came back for a second square go at the queers the people holding their jacket would as likely come from Scotland's left as its right, or that they'd be backed in their bigotry by some of the richest and most powerful people on the planet.

As we now know, Scotland's queer utopia was short-lived. Two and a half decades after Keep The Clause failed, the millionaire who bankrolled it has the ear of the Deputy First Minister, an evangelical who came very close to landing the top job; political parties have dropped their years-long pledges to ban conversion therapy and now promise to enact additional harms against trans people instead; the media once again frames eliminationist views and hateful speech as the respectable views in a reasonable debate.

While hate crimes against the entire community continue to rise, the media and ministers tell the nation to fear the victims of hate, not the people purveying it. And when you listen to the callers and contributors to Scots radio shows or read the columnists and commenters on Scots newspaper websites, something becomes clear: if the Section 28 ballot were happening today, too many of our politicians, public figures and peers would be voting to keep it.

This is why the stickerer is not afraid.

Our existence is a problem, they say. And they're right, although they're wrong about the why. Our existence isn't a problem to the wider world; we are a threat to no one, and we could no more turn straight kids queer or cis kids trans than conversion therapy, hate crimes and shitty healthcare have managed to turn queer kids straight or trans kids cis.

But we *are* a problem for the bigots. Seeing us hurts their eyes, and it hurts all the more when they see us thrive. Our joy, our laughter and our love are an inconvenient truth that makes a mockery of everything they say about us, a truth that exposes them as the very demons they tell others to fear. They may pretend to be angels and promise protection, but they are devils hell-bent on elimination.

Our existence makes that clear. Our existence shows that they, not we, are the impostors; that they, not we, are the ones pretending to be something they are not; that they, not we, are a danger to others.

They are snake oil sellers, and the bullshit they bottle is a a fiction that claims to be non-fiction, a cynical concoction of fake facts and false narratives, a cocktail of cruelty whose ingredients include not one atom of evidence. But our lives, our experiences, our happiness… that's evidence, and it exposes the fraud.

That's why they fight so hard to ensure that the people they denigrate and demonise cannot be permitted to tell their own stories, to ensure that our community is constantly talked about but never listened to. We must be silenced, shuttered, sent back to the closet, because if we are able to share our stories then people will discover that none of the tales they're being told about us are true.

That silencing might have been possible in the 1980s, when a single clause could—did—cut off our entire community. But we weren't so quiet in 2000, and we're louder and prouder now. There are too many of us walking unafraid now, not just surviving but thriving.

As American essayist Ralph Waldo Emerson put it: 'The mind, once stretched by a new idea, never returns to its original dimensions.' Our existence is that idea. The bigots can do their worst, and God knows they will try. But the queer genie is out of the bottle and they are never going back in.

The stickerer is already lost, because the cult she has fallen into will strip every last layer of her life until only the cult remains. We can't save her, even if we wanted to. But what we can do, what we should do, is to do to the cults what they so want to do to us: marginalise them, mock them and make them ashamed—not just for queer people's sakes, but for all marginalised people. We are canaries in the coal mine, warning of even worse trouble to come.

If you're an LGBTQ+ ally, that means we need you to do more than stand with us and affirm us online. Allyship is a thing you do, not a thing that you are, and what we need you to do is to actively stand against those who hate and want to harm. We need you to do it proudly, to do it loudly, to make it clear that no space is a safe space for bigotry no matter how politely spoken. For all our sakes, we need you to make bigots afraid again.

The anti-gender, anti-feminist, anti-queer movement believes that it has turned the tide of progress permanently. It's time to show them what they really are: a bunch of Cnuts who, like that much-maligned monarch, cannot and will not stop the tide from roaring back.

Colin McGuire

FRUIT POTENTIAL

Queen

'There is rapidly deepening public alarm over the deadly disease.' The announcement catches me off guard as I walk by the living room. The door is open. The TV on. I peer in to make sure the room is empty before walking in and sitting on the arm of the couch, eyes fixed on the screen. It's a report about something awful, a sickness killing men, something that means they are bad in some way. They show footage of Freddie Mercury. Freddie has the disease too. Freddie Mercury scares me. His sickness scares me.

The way Freddie looks as he sings is like the sickness itself is singing. He looks like how I imagine a witch might: thin, bony fingers, long black hair, a pale complexion and a gaunt face. But this witch has bright buck teeth and is in an ice white jump suit, pining for his Mum in 'Bohemian Rhapsody.'

The song scares me too, its high-pitched emotion unsettles me. I want to change the channel, turn it off, part of me wants to keep watching. Don't tell anyone anything.

After the news an advert comes on. It shows a volcano erupting, rock collapsing, volcanic flames and lava bubbling and pouring. A man with a large pneumatic drill drills into the rock as a disembodied hand chips at it with a hammer and chisel. Over ominous synths a stern voice warns, 'There is a danger that has become a threat to us all. It is a deadly disease and there is no known cure.' A huge black tombstone is lowered from a black sky with the word AIDS in bold white carved into it. It lies flat on the ground while unseen mourners throw white flowers on it. 'Don't die of ignorance,' the voice intones.

My body tenses and strains. Palms itch. Mind races. I know this is Freddie's disease, the disease that he is. This is the disease we share in common. This is who I am and what I will die from. No more nakedness with the boy next door. No more bodies pressed together. There is a sickness taking over the world, a real-life horror film, and I am not even old enough to watch horror films yet.

The advert and Freddie make my horror. I have to get out of here, away from the TV, away from the boy next door, away from my own nakedness and disease potential.

I will have to ask Mum if I have it. I don't exactly know what AIDS is, but I know it's a bug in the blood that makes the blood bad. Freddie Mercury is AIDS. I am Freddie Mercury's double. I am sickly and skeletal. I get naked with the boy in the cellar. We press our bodies together.

First Confession

I lock myself in the bathroom, pace in circles, eyes red, hands shaking. What am I going to do? Mum and Dad will reject me. My brother will hate me.

Imagine the whole extended family finding out. The humiliation.

I could run. I could end it.

No one can know about any of this. I don't want to admit this, I couldn't admit it, what would it be like to say it? Would they see me differently? Would I be able to get back who I was before? Why is it so hard to admit secret things? The urge to confess at odds with an impulse to hide.

I want to stay here, but the pressure from the tears and confusion forces me to move, I can't handle it alone. I'm only eight. Somebody needs to tell me what to do. All I can do right now is stay here and pace.

Mum knocks on the door. 'Are you OK in there?' I say yes, tears streaming down my face. Yes, I'm fine. But she knows I'm not. She insists I open; I am not ready to. I want the door shut. I feel safer with it closed, like a confessional box, a divide between priest and sinner. 'Well, I'll be in my room if you need me,' she says.

When eventually I am ready to go, having grown sick of the walls, I unlock the snib and walk to my parents' bedroom flushed and drained from fear.

We kneel at opposite sides of the bed, like a nun and a choirboy at prayer, I struggle to speak, choked with emotion. 'You can tell me anything, Colin. We love you,' she reassures me. Shame makes it feel unspeakable, a weight stuck in the throat just below my Adam's apple, but finally, as if a crowbar had been placed inside my mouth and wedged it out, I speak. People do these sorts of things, she says. It is normal. Natural. Friends do these sorts of things with friends. Boys do these things. Girls too. Everyone.

But I don't feel comforted by that. It's not that Mum is incapable of supporting me, but that no amount of soothing can convince me that it is OK. Now that the secret has been launched out in to the world, I am left exposed. Have I been too honest? I can't take it back now. What I've said can't be unsaid. I had declassified it, and, in an instant, wanted it classified again.

Cellar Door

We sit in the cool, dimly lit cellar to escape from the sun, drinking from plastic cups of water. Having checked that the door is shut, out of boredom or restlessness we begin to nudge elbows into ribs, flick hair and splash water in each other's faces. My shirt gets wet, so I take it off and throw it in his face, flexing my arms and chest like a wrestler. He looks at me, scrunching his eyes slightly. He takes off his T-shirt too.

I pick up a thin white sheet splattered with paint stains, wrap it around my bare shoulders, wafting it and gusting it like a cape. He drapes himself in a sheet too. We snake around the cellar, spin in and out of rooms, our feet bare and dirty from the dust and grit on the ground. We climb on top of boxes, catching and escaping each other's grasp, our skins brushing as we pass; on the boundary of something we can't quite name. The tails of the sheets caress our chests as they sweep through the air.

We undress to underwear only, pressing chests together as we pass, feeling the warmth through the thinness of the sheet. I open my sheet wide like a bird, displaying my smooth bare body. He presses against me as I wrap the sheet around us, pressing close through our underwear, feeling the surprise of another boy's skin against mine.

There are footsteps outside. The cellar door opens, light streaming in and straining our eyes. 'What are you lads up to?' his dad asks, surprised. As his eyes adjust to the darkness he sees us in our pants, draped in white. 'Get your clothes on, won't you?' he says. 'It's cold down here, get out into the sun.' We laugh, shy, our clothes thrown in a heap on the old couch. We decide to go outside, naked. We run unafraid, draped in sheets, our cherubic buttocks flashing in the garden.

'Is this OK?' I ask his mum about our nakedness. She's pegging the last of the washing, barely taking note. 'Yes, it's fine,' she says brightly. His dad comes out of the cellar with the hose and makes his way up the drive to wash the car. We swirl and bump together, flitting in and out of a green plastic *He-Man and the Masters of the Universe* tent pitched in the grass, and dart back in and out of the cellar too.

I pick up a policeman's hat from the dress up box and put it on. I stand proudly, one leg on the edge of the couch and my arm in the air. 'You're under arrest—for having no clothes on!' I say, pointing at him. 'Catch me first and dress me yourself,' he says, turning and ducking behind the dress up box. He finds another police hat and puts it on. 'Let's arrest everyone for having clothes on!' he laughs. 'It's illegal to get dressed!'

We charge out into the sun, yelling.

Salmon Farming in Argyle and Bute

This isn't a coming out email. It is a quick, avoidant, hiding away email.

Mum knows anyway. Has done for years, ever since I locked myself in the toilet, ever since I asked her if I had AIDS, and told her about the boy next door.

As if it weren't bleak enough here, deep in the frozen winter on a salmon farm on the West Coast of Scotland. And yet here I am talking about my sexuality over email. I want to avoid the whole subject, and I cringe as I type the word 'gay'. It doesn't fit. It fits just right.

That's the issue.

Ambivalence.

I have to get back to the hatchery anyway. Lunch is over.

From: Colin
To: Mum
Subject: (no subject)
Date: Thur, 11th Jan 2007, 12:49.

Hey Mum,

Got your letter—was good to receive—unexpected.

My virus stayed with me for a few days. My throat became hellishly sore, but it eventually went away but I then made several other people quite ill.

I'm enjoying working up here (in the middle of nowhere) with big hearty lunches and lots of work it's all good. Literally get up at 7 every morning, work through till 5, go home, wash, read, write, sing, dance, eat, have a few beers now and then and then go to bed and start all over again. Still worth it for the money and experience.

I'll be back in Glasgow on Sat. I'll call you to say hello.

O, I should mention this, no big deal, don't say anything, I'm confident I'm gay. No need to go wild or anything but I just felt I should mention it. Don't make a big deal out of it or talk about it. Ha-ha. And I'll see you when I return.

Talk soon
Your loving son colin :) x

Salmon eggs are a delicacy. The best ones are disinfected, stored and then sold to restaurants. The very best ones are sold to other hatcheries around the world to breed better strains of salmon.

To produce the eggs, brood fish are kept together, three females to one male. Particular attention is paid to breeding the very best male fish. The female salmon are called spawners, and when they get spawned hundreds of eggs gush from their torn bellies in a cascade of orange balls, then they are euthanised.

The eggs are tiny orange balls with black dots inside them that look like an eyelash, or pubic hair, or a seed trapped inside.

We count salmon eggs in the hatchery all day long, separating the clear orange eggs from the impure, the congealed and mouldy. We wear wellington boots, white coats, hats and scarves to insulate against the cold and wet.

The hatchery is brightly lit, clinical white, like a science lab or a medical department where busy med doctors work with strange diseases, but the floor is flushed with water. The eggs are stored in white buckets on metal shelving around the room. To keep the eggs fresh and at the correct temperature, cold water is channelled from a series of hosepipes which hang from the walls and run into the buckets.

We sit around a large metallic table that has a trough in the middle that water washes through. The buckets sit on small stands down the centre of the table and are connected to hoses. We spoon the eggs into little sieves and sift through them with plastic tweezers.

Salmon farming offers me the essentials: escape, money, booze and weed. I work with some English guys and Polish guys, some women from Australia and New Zealand, and guys from Ireland and India.

I like it here. I am far from Glasgow, far from my normal crowd and routine, far from the deep cringe of my sexuality and my never-ending misunderstanding.

Skinhead

Here I am, balls deep in winter in a room full of Polish skinheads.

We—me, Pawel, Sebastian, Bartek and Tomek—have gone to Tomek's cabin for a night of music, weed and vodka. We share joints and pour shots, each shot chased with a drink of beer. We drink fiercely. We drink to get smashed.

We pass around cheap Mayfair cigarettes. Bartek rolls a joint. Sebastian too. The resin is blackened around the edges. I did that. I'm no dealer, but I'd been give the job of transporting half a nine-bar up to the estate on one of my recent runs back to Glasgow. I microwaved the hash to soften it for cutting and ended up burning the resin, carrying it on the bus like a bag of burnt brownies. There are no complaints: it stains our fingers charcoal black but it's still good enough to smoke.

Pawel doesn't smile much. He has a shaved head and a serious stare; he is not long out of Polish jail but what he did I don't know, and I don't ask. Sebastian and Bartek's heads are shaved too.

They look like a table of convicts, or prisoners of war.

We are starting to get drunk now. My throat burns from drinking straight shot after straight shot and smoking packed, harsh joints.

A few weeks before coming to the farm I celebrated Hogmanay in Glasgow, kissing boys on the Art School dance floor. That inspired me to come out at the farm in a haphazard way. They don't seem to care, but I do. I drink and smoke my shame and my insecurity, hiding by being the loudest one in the room.

Tonight I am an agent provocateur, asking for trouble. I am lairy. 'I'm a gay straight bisexual pansexual asexual omnisexual man. I love all people,' I declare. 'I love all people!' I mimic and mock Tomek's mannerisms and voice. 'You're definitely gay, Tomek!'

I goad Pawel—'Ever kissed a guy, Pawel?'—and flick douts at Tomek's head. He laughs and throws them back. 'Bloody bastard,' he says. Bloody bastard is the name he likes to call me.

Things are simmering. My adrenalin fizzes and my vision blurs. I want something to happen, to party, to dance. I want release, but I don't know how to get it, I want some chaos.

I take over the music and demand we listen to The Knife's queer Swedish electro; demand we watch the video to 'Pass This On', on Tomek's laptop. The video shows a group of men and women of different ages and ethnicities in a bar that looks like a cabin. They are drinking beers and smoking, looking gloomy. The young men have skinheads, wear tracksuits; the old men smoke with stern expressions. It cuts to a pair of legs and reveals that they belong to a beautiful drag queen. She turns up the volume and lets the music blare.

As she dances and sings, it's unclear whether the people in the cabin are comfortable: will they accept her or will they kick off, and demand she stop, disgusted by her overt display of sexuality? One of the skinheads approaches her—but instead of attacking her, he dances. The ice is broken, the barriers lifted, and soon everyone is dancing. It ends with a close-up of one of the young women, her stare a question mark.

'Again, again!' I demand. I love it. Its provocation. I love the way it moves from awkwardness and uncertainty to acceptance and celebration. It is a portal into a different kind of world.

'There is only sexuality!' I shout. 'A gay straight bi pan bisexual reality!'

The boys look confused but unbothered, so I change the subject. 'George Orwell finished *1984* on the Isle of Jura, just across the water! It's a conspiracy!'

I demand a haircut. 'At 2am?' Tomek says. Yes. Full skin head, I say. I want to join my Polish brothers.

Tomek goes to get his shaver and takes my skull to the bone. I look sinister, a punk, a neo-Nazi, Olof from The Knife, Jimmy Somerville from Bronski Beat, Annie Lennox from Eurhythmics. I could give a Nazi salute or kiss a man. I could be a Pole, or a POW.

We knock back more vodka as Tomek drunkenly sweeps up my hair from the floor. Polish metal is playing in the background, the singer shouting 'Spierdalaj!'—in English, 'fuck off'—over and over. We are all lairy now. We fling shots in our faces instead of downing them. I wrestle Pawel and Sebastian. They pin me down. I kick out, thrash, part play, part carnal. In our drunkenness we are on the brink, the place where play fights can become bloody noses. We crash into the table, knocking bottles, ashtrays and half-built joints onto the carpet. 'Bloody Bastard, that's enough,' Tomek shouts, turning the music off.

It's time to leave. I can barely stand up straight.

I'm pushed out the door and stagger across the path to my cabin.

~

In the morning I am slumped on the couch in a living room thick with smoke. The other lodgers are running around, opening windows, clearing the air. Paul is in oven gloves, carrying a hot tray with a smoking, carbonised meteorite of a pepperoni pizza on it. Clearly, I had started cooking before passing out.

'Colin! Are you nuts, mate!?' he says. 'You could have set the cabin on fire!'

'You look like a Nazi with that skinhead,' he says disapprovingly. 'Come on. We've got work in thirty minutes.'

Mae Diansangu

VI. THE LOVERS

There is a God-less Eden
where queer beasts blossom.
A wet monster with two hearts,
four hands, and sixty-four teeth,
whispers love in twin speak.
Eve calls Lilith daddy, then one day
her other half asks to be renamed—
I think I might be a man.
Ten fingers sink into the dirt,
searching for a new sound.
They pull two syllables from
the dust. Eve thrusts the name
of The First Man inside her.
The lovers fast their hands
with a golden serpent.
Amber promises fuse
their wrists together.
They ask the snake to father
their children. Two bellies
swell with choices and their
consequences. Eve rests
an apple on her husband's
baby bump. A little kick
is all it takes to set things
in motion, to un-bid
the forbidden

Mae Diansangu

XVIII. THE MOON

She sucks the shadow

out from under us,

kisses the grubby miracle

of our body.

Her tongue can see

in the dark, but it blinds our joyless 'I'.

We scratch at moonburt skin,

dirtying our fingernails

with dreams.

Anxiety and intuition

feel the same when

they move inside us—

we trust her to illuminate

the path, so we don't

have to gaslight

our way home.

Her light reflects

what we already know.

Mae Diansangu

XX. JUDGEMENT

Whenever the sky wasn't looking, I tried my best
to get away with what I could. Hid the the messy
and the strange, made the unchangeable invisible.
But nothing could soften the blow, or slacken
the rhythm of resurrection, at precisely 2.47am
in the Broxdon Roundabout McDonald's—
when Gabriel's horn rattled the walls.
The trumpet's voice pulled three identical faces
out from behind the one I always wore in public,
slammed them together, forced them to look
at each other. Sticky melodies leaked from
the broken McFlurry machine, the angel's song
pooled at my feet. Soon I was knee deep in shame.
A whole life forgetting every name I was made
to live up to. An orchestra of bones clicked
underground. The sound of them knitting together
scraped the enamel off my teeth. At last, my mouth
could hear the lesson the dead have to teach:
the womb and the grave are the same shape.
Heavy with music, I limped towards the exit.
The World sighed behind the door.
The me I could no longer ignore
pushed it wide open.

Lakshmi Ajay

RECLAIM, RETREAT, RESCUE

i used to think that my queerness was what chased me away from my home/land, searching for safety;
a place to breathe;
as me

The first time I arrived at Munro's Island,
—Mundrothuruthu as the locals call it—I
was a tourist in my own land.

Our waves sway back and forth, feeling the mud beneath us slip
away and only to return to our fold.
We remember a time when this land was hidden deep in our
bosom, untouched by man.

My family had chosen one of the newest additions
to the hotels on the island to stay in; gleaming white
concrete towering amongst the small coloured
brick houses that flecked the rest of the island.

I had tea in the morning, served by a young girl
from her shack attached to her bright blue house.

97

That girl dives into our salty embrace every morning.

The shame of that concrete whiteness
descended upon me as I stomped around the
island—each footfall pushing the Sinking
Island further into the surrounding water.

> *Year after year, the mould we spawned plagues her*
> *breath and threads its way through her clothes.*

> *Her neighbours flee when they tire of waking up*
> *knee deep in us on their porches.*

> *She knows her blue house is next.*

> *She loves the fireworks on the pier*
> *at the turn of the year;*
> *we've loved watching those sparks reflected in*
> *her eyes over the years*
> *as we creep forward across the low lying pier.*

The heavy grief of displacement/
of leaving/
of returning/
of never belonging/
all rippled through me as I wept into my
lovers' arms by the shores of the salty lake.

I wept through my desperate bids for
connection to my blood and land.

A stranger to this land sits weeping by the shore.
We greet your tears gently,
your salt; the same as ours; the same as hers.

Each tear
carried the sorrows of those who chose to
stay and those who had to flee the island,
of all those who have felt the force of
colonisers and capitalists ravaging their land.

The grief of your loss is nothing compared
to the devastation of ours.

The lives within us have been fenced
off by their nets, their factories,
the canoes full of gawkers and mounds of waste
from their resorts.

The fireworks this year are ours.
We will push them back into our depths.

but now,

**as i straddle the two islands that made me,
i wonder how my queerness has helped me
trans/form as i move through these spaces**

I have visited Mundrothuruthu several times
since that New Years' morning.

*Take take take, that's all they do.
Man, woman, child, creature—*

Munro arrived on our shore in 1812.

*He is still lauded as the man that claimed our land for men,
still celebrated*

*for his 'gift' of this fertile soil
—islands still named after him, walls of museums and galleries
crown him,
and boxed up classrooms praising his railroads.*

As I sit in my solid brick and mortar home on another
island, listening to raindrops lashing against my windowsill,

I think of this girl, who didn't get to tell me her name,
and I think of the Scot, John Munro. The coloniser, who
retreated to Teaninich Castle after reclaiming the island
from the Ashtamudi Lake.

Munro dredged up soil from the bottom of the lake,
mixed it with cement to form the perfect mound—a
brand new creation to mark on his map of conquest.

They left us ravaged by their greedy fingers.
Fingers that come from afar.
Fingers ungentle.
Fingers that believe
a mere man can be their salvation.

They broke our backs with the weight of
their metal train lines,
their industry,
their insurmountable greed.

I think of the residents of Mundrothuruthu and the floods that devastate them every monsoon season.

I see the girl that served me tea one New Year's morning, and imagine salt water laying waste to her tea stall and her livelihood.

I map Munro's final home, Teaninich Castle, only 3 hours and 15 minutes away from where I live now. Mundrothuruthu is more than a day's journey by flight.

We might seem like a vastness that they can
simply twist into a pretzel ready for the selling.

Human time does not work the way ours does.
Their lives are a minuscule of our existence; yet
in that second, they have pillaged us.

When does an emigrant start to feel like a
tourist—removed and unaffected

When does a tourist become a neo/
coloniser—only taking and never giving

this land belongs to no wo/man, but us
and it will return
only to us

We saw Munro several years later by the
shores of Cromarty Firth, bent over with the
scars of age.

Gold that he pillaged from our land streaked
across the walls of his lofty castle in the
highlands.
Flashing before us were the splotches of mould
that will soon cling to the coloured houses he
raised on the island.

We call upon wind, rain and storm
When we transform
One day, his castle will be ours too.

i think of how our land never belonged
to man
but
to the water
the earth

Where is their humanity? Be ready to see ours.

*They dive into our depth looking for cockles but
they will come up empty handed.*

*This land was never his to claim; never his to exploit.
So now we take it back.
As droves of tourists flood to holiday on the sinking
island, we flood the soil polluting it with our salt.*

*When will they stop?
Only when it is no more;*

reclaimed by us

**my queerness transcends norms, borders
and empires to be with a stranger that
made me tea from across the world
to be with the water that borne me.**

the tea stall that she built is still standing.

Shola von Reinhold

NOVEL FRAGMENT

Opal waited as the Natural Philosopher visited the lavatory. By the wall nearest her was a kind of vitrine. It looked very old. Attached to it by a string threaded through a drilled hole was a grey metal coin, maybe pewter, its faces rubbed down and indeterminate. She dropped it in the slot and a light came on in the box.

'The most recent are disappointments... works of... clearly a... tawdry period of the rebis cults...'

'But ma'am, would you... illuminations are...'

'Vulgarities... of the same ilk as that...'

The machine clanked and a curtain jerked open. A dirge dribbled from some interior music box—tuneless bells with many gaps entirely in whatever tune was meant to play.

But what Grotto saw when the curtain opened unsettled her.

A glittering diorama—an artificial pastoral—it literally, materially, twinkled—green velveted hills, studded all over with flecks and chips of crystal.

Or perhaps it settled, not unsettled, something inside her. Something inside her became motionless as it moved.

It moved—the painted sky—like those in opera—like those painted backdrops all over the world—moved and became cloud-covered—grey clouds shimmering beneath dusty crystal beads, and then a wooded scene framed in mountains… the sky receded and caves appeared. Visible was a cliff of caves…also studded with crystals or tiny seed shells, whorled grottos… one glimpsed a kind of resin in a cave mouth: pseudo-water gleamed. Then the light in the box flickered and went off. A green light came on. From one grotto, by a concealed mechanical string or track, emerged a waxen figurine. where the wax had been moulded into breast, the pigmentation had, mysteriously, all but turned transparent, but for the areola—green. Verdigris.

'Oh but the grande finale…' The Natural Philosopher had returned. Another strange chime gave out and from between the figure's legs protruded a violet-tipped priapus.

This made the professor laugh.

It was supposed, she thought, to be amusing, pornographic perhaps, lewd, but she thought the whole thing… She recalled, vividly, the feeling she'd had in the borough: the roofs, the green breath driven up by the rain.

Suki Hollywood

HOLIER THAN THOU

The historical fact that Jesus and Judas were born in Palestine is necessary to assert, particularly as this work of fancy was written during Israel's ongoing genocide of Palestinians.

From the river to the sea, Palestine will be free.

The house party that Judas was hiding from was heaving with faces he knew from apps and illegal club nights and his hairdresser's Instagram. Still, his link to the crowd was tenuous; Matty, the host, was the fag to his sister's hag. Matty, with Gemma's help, had been trying to get with Judas all night, but he worked for the Lib Dems (too far, even for Judas).

Judas didn't know anyone else there—or knew them too well—so he stood in his clothing like a silhouette in the clean-carpeted living room, cigarette dangling from his lips. He was waiting for someone to drink enough to decide that one smoke wouldn't kill them and ask him for one.

Finally, a blonde opened up the circle to absorb Judas. He looked like he'd change out of his mesh top on Monday to touch base and circle back; he looked like he'd been born in a hospital.

'I like your hat,' he said. English. Of course. 'Very Lavender Country. Have you heard of them? They're this amazing queer group from the seventies.'

Judas was not queer. Queer was too polite, educated and querulous a word. Judas was gay. It was meatier and more universal, if a little uncomfortably Kurt from *Glee*. He was a homo. He was a FAG. But, yes, he told Peter—not Pete, he noted with heavy dread, but conclusively Peter—he had heard of Lavender Country.

'Oh, sick,' Peter said. The phrase was sudden in his mouth, as though he'd seen it written down but had never said it before. 'How about The Four Horsemen? They're from the nineties, super underrated. The lead singer died—'

Seeing where this was going, Judas excused himself to the bathroom before it became obvious that he didn't really like country music, just the clothes.

Judas flicked the brim of his cowboy hat with a roguish wink and looked at the strange angel in the mirror. Crisp black shirt, held together at the collar with a silk scarf, cherry red and so fine it was verging liquid. His mouth was soured with tobacco, but he sweetened his lips with Kool-Aid flavoured balm (like Irn-Bru, but American and therefore Ethel Cain-adjacent). His jeans shaped his skinny legs into weapons, something that could flex, pantherlike.

Clip clop, his boots snapped on his re-entry to the party which had not noticed his exit.

'Alright, troops?' he announced. It is Britney, bitch.

Triumphantly, he lit up his cigarette at last, but there was nothing to tap except his own Budweiser bottle. He kept missing the mouth of it, and ash landed on the carpet like smashed eyeshadow. Judas didn't vape for the same reason he called himself a FAG: he was nothing if not committed and had a proudly monogamous heart. When he explained this to a software engineer in a harness also getting a beer from the fridge, the guy laughed and said, 'Yeah'.

Gemma and Matty were doing lines from the surface of a mirror in a bedroom, which felt to symbolically on the nose for Judas. The group Peter was sitting with seemed indignant about the latest situation; Judas could tell by their charity shop outfits and the face masks a couple of them wore as they turned to look at him.

The masks made Judas think of the pest, which made him feel angry (didn't want to think of the pest) and guilt (hadn't done a test for the pest though Matty had asked everyone to).

'Anyone want a beer?' Judas asked, blowing smoke through his nose. 'You'll have to take your mask off to drink it, though.'

'I'll take one,' one said, removing his mask and letting his long hair loose.

Like all of us, Judas had seen this person before. During the last lockdown, he'd gone to the public toilets of the park. He had no experience of cruising, so followed urban legend instructions as if he'd read them in an ancient tome.

Jesus had been waiting in the dark cubicle. His nose was freshly pierced, his pockets full of wild garlic. Judas didn't know at that point that he was going to kill him, but he knew he was going to kiss him. Jesus hissed when he did: his wound was tender.

With his mouth, Judas had asked Jesus, Can you tell me how to be good? And Jesus had said, You are. And then again, with a bite on his bottom lip that drew blood, You are!

Judas opened Jesus' beer with his teeth and passed it to him. It was as if the place where the two of them were standing had been touched by lightning once, and had never forgotten what it felt like.

The conversation was on daddies. 'My father was a fisherman,' Peter said. 'Now he manages a fleet of trawlers and still calls himself working class.'

Matty's father was rich and, according to Gemma, hot.

'Corporate daddy,' she said.

'He's evil,' Matty said

'Evil is hot,' Gemma said. 'Like a mean cop, you know. You don't want to marry him or whatever, but you want him to fuck you.'

That night Judas had a dream his dad handed him a handwritten note that either read APOLOGISE or APOLOGY. It was forgotten as he coughed awake, naked on Gemma's sofa.

He must have slept with his mouth wide open because his tongue was dry and dead. Rubbing it with his finger, back and forth, Judas thought of the beauty spot at the corner of Jesus' mouth, like a crumb he hadn't licked away yet.

Had Jesus remembered him? Judas didn't know. Gemma had started vomiting into Matty's coat closet before he could do much more than brush their gazes.

'She'll be fine,' Judas had said, even while Matty was watching the Uber arrive in-app and handing Judas his fringed jacket.

Maybe, he consoled himself, it was good that he had been aloof, mysterious, slippery by leaving early. Last time, Jesus had left first, and Judas had felt the shame of telling someone who has cooked you dinner that you're still hungry.

He reached for his phone. He'd followed the chain of mutuals from Gemma to Matty to Jesus last night. At 5am Judas had reshared a photograph of an America road sign.

ARE YOU GOING TO COWBOY UP OR LIE THERE AND BLEED?

At 5:03am he'd reshared a text post.

RELEASE THE VACCINES. FREE HEALTHCARE NOW.

Jesus hadn't watched it yet; hadn't even started following Judas back yet.

Gemma's mouth was slack against the pillow. The room was white and dirty: floor snarled with clothes and empty bottles of Diet Coke, an ashtray and a mixing bowl full of vomit within reach of the bed. Cat litter crunched under his feet. The cat only felt safe enough to piss in Gemma's bedroom. Judas pulled a twenty-pound note from her handbag and rolled three cigarettes before she woke up.

Judas broke the twenty to get a steak bake from Greggs. The steam when he bit into it was like the hot breath of a dog. He ordered an espresso, too. The cig and the little paper espresso cup were in his right hand, phone in his left, as if he was busy and on the clock. He hoped he looked like an Italian waiter, or—equally chic—a personal assistant in New York.

Judas refreshed the app. Jesus still hadn't added him back, but Peter (ugh) had watched his story. Judas hate-watched Peter's story: a photo of a group of people with protest signs outside Cathedral Street Hospital.

SIMON'S STORY: Get down if you can! + hot selfie (for the algo).

JUDAS: YES!!! SHUD I BRING ANYTHING?

The subway wormed through the city with an orange rattle. Everyone on it dripped on the seats. Judas hated taking the subway. He feared being trapped in an enclosed space with football fans. None today. Just other unemployed people, the mothers, the elderly, and the inpested.

He opened his phone. Jesus had still not followed him back, but then, there was no signal down here. Judas let his head loll, the subway rocking him like a sleep deprived mother.

Jesus' eyes had flicked between Judas and Gemma's shared face as she'd described Papa Iscariot. Estranged, she said. Estrangement was too a bloodless word to do the job; they were nothing so possible as strangers.

Jesus didn't know anything about his father, he told them, sipping his beer, except he saved people from fires. Or did he set them? Something like that anyway: there were people and there were fires, and his father came into it somehow.

'Excuse me, pet?'

Judas cracked an eye open. The compartment was empty now, except for himself and an old woman in a wee anorak. He was at the same stop he'd got on at. The Glasgow subway was an ouroboros, chasing its tail until the service stopped.

'Yeah?' he said, bristling and ready to be ineffectively hate-crimed.

'Lend us your lighter?' she asked, an unlit cigarette already in her hand.

He stared. 'This is the subway,' he said.

'I know that,' she replied. Her drawn-on eyebrows were blue.

Okay. Party. 'Here,' he said, flicking open his classic kerosene silver vintage-style lighter (Ali Express).

She breathed out huffs of grey smoke until the compartment was as dense as a speakeasy. Worried that she wanted to talk to him, Judas looked at his phone.

SIMON: Water is good to bring, but orange juice is better.
JUDAS: OK BITZ OR NO BITZ

When she was halfway through, the woman said something Judas couldn't hear over the scream of the subway.

'What?' he said, flicking his lighter open and shut in his hand.

Her eyes were bloodshot from smoke. 'I'm going to die in three months. The pest,' she said.

'Oh,' he said. 'Fuck. Sorry.'

'I'm not going to a lazaretto,' she said. 'I'm going to die in my own sitting room, in the same chair as daddy.'

'Sure,' Judas said. 'That makes sense.'

Judas arrived with his arms full of orange juice cartons (with bits). He looked up and down the line for Simon, but everyone looked the same in dark masks, anoraks and hoodies. Judas turned a few heads, as if people were unsure of the motivations of his cowboy hat.

Baa! he thought as he nodded, the buckle of his belt glinting like a silver dollar. *Baa!*

The hospital protests had been happening sporadically since the last public hospital closed three years ago. Like most hospitals, this one had become a private facility, primarily dealing in pest vaccines. Judas had never attended, as a paying customer or a protestor. The posts online claimed the protests were run by workers, but the accounts he saw share them were mostly poets or art school graduates from London with skinny arses and funding, with a healthy smattering of trans fem DJs.

Judas finally spotted Simon in *Hackers* (1995) fingerless gloves and, honest to god, combat trousers. He was talking intently with someone in waterproof trousers and walking boots, presumably planning to bag a Munro after this.

Simon was an artist, from London, with funding. Judas liked him, but wished he would admit painting was a hobby he used to scam institutions. Judas was a believer in the people's coin. He wasn't an artist, but if he was he'd make money by genuinely selling shit and the day he couldn't he'd get a real job, like a plumber or whatever.

'Hi. I brought orange juice,' Judas said significantly, holding out a carton.

'No thanks,' Peter, the Munro bagger, said. 'I hate bits.'

Simon was so thrilled to see him that Judas knew it was only a matter of time before he unironically addressed him as comrade. But Simon knew Peter and Peter knew Jesus, so Judas cheerfully held up a sign that said PRIVATE HEALTHCARE KILLS! Between chants, he chatted with those around him about the rev, which he agreed was sure to come, any day now.

Some passing public tooted their horns, or raised a fist in tired camaraderie, but for the most part, the message of a better world slapped up against dull apathy like a bird against a fresh window. Judas did appreciate the hateful comments, however;

- 'Get a job!' a man out of his car window (a classic).
- 'Those people are animals,' a woman with a shitzu on a lead muttered to her companion. 'A few weeks ago, they yelled in my dog's FACE' (huge if true).
- 'Rats,' one young man in a suit gave them. 'Diseased lefty tramps! Sexual deviants!' (Judas planned to write this with a sharpie on a T-shirt).
- 'Blood on your hands,' a man in a Tesla said authoritatively, his wife in the passenger seat in a mask.
- Maybe his wife needed the vax. Maybe, it was her third or fourth getting the pest and one more time would kill her.
- It wasn't her fault she could pay for it and other people couldn't.
- if he could pay to never get the pest again, he would.
- who wouldn't?

Meanwhile, the facility managers waited inside their electric cars, watching. The police spoke quietly on their radios, comments that the protesters couldn't hear. It was Pride month, so their shoulders were decorated with regulation rainbows.

An hour passed. There was no sign of Jesus. Someone ran up and down the line to warn them that things were about to escalate. Judas didn't know what that meant; he had also just taken a bite of a wet roasted vegetable sandwich so couldn't ask.

'No shame if you need to leave,' Simon said. 'There is a possibility of arrest.'

Judas was still chewing when a new brigade of police arrived around the corner.

'Everyone link!' someone shouted, but it was too late.

The police speared into the picket line: bodies hard as splinters, tearing the protesters apart from each other like limpets from a rock. As he was roughly jostled, Judas dropped his sandwich and wished he'd worn something with more pockets (like combat trousers).

In the crush, someone grabbed Judas' hand. Judas willingly held it, and even gave them a squeeze to say solidarity, comrade! Then the hand pulled away with second-hand embarrassment, Judas realised that they'd wanted to link arms instead, and was further mortified to realise the hand belonged to Jesus.

With his arm in Judas' elbow, Jesus drew them tight as a stitch and Judas was woven into the fabric of the picket line even while he was still Humming and Hahing over if he was truly willing to be arrested. Jesus didn't ask him, he was gazing at the horizon of horsed police officers approaching. It was too late. Clip clop, clip clop.

Once they were behind them, the cops turned their bodies the same direction as the picket line, like a second row of shark teeth. Protestors, pulling each-other up, started to chant, All Cops are Bastards! All Cops are Bastards! Judas could feel the bulk of the man behind him, belted equipment pressing into his lower back. A cop's elbow already digging into Jesus' shoulder.

I would die for you, Judas thought, as Jesus pinned his long, dark hair up with a butterfly claw clip, one-handed. Please ask me to die for you.

'Doing alright there?' a cop behind Jesus called to another.

'Just another day in the office!'

'Just another day of this shite when we could be saving lives,' another chimed in.

Judas got the sense that this camaraderie was for their benefit. His suspicion was confirmed when the first cop tried to draw them into conversation.

'Why do you need to shout that?' he asked, as though hurt. 'We're right here. Why don't you talk to us?'

'What was that?' Simon said. 'Oink oink?'

Judas found the cops faceless and dull, as though the uniform bleached them of all character save citizenship. Trying to ignore that they were behind him, he closed his eyes.

'You okay, cowboy?' Jesus asked him.

Judas turned to look at him. His eyes were brown, in a burning kind of way. He wore a red keffiyeh; Judas wondered where he was from, and how to find out without coming off as racist.

'Yeah,' Judas said. 'You?'

The cop behind Jesus dug his elbow in deeper, as if marking him.

'Doing okay,' he said, face tense. 'We'll be alright.'

There was a jolt, spread up the line like a ripple. A police officer was hauling someone away: a doll Judas recognised from clubs, dressed in a beige hoodie and scrunchie with the studied comfort of a K-pop star's airport outfit. She was screaming. A ribbon of others ran after the two, tightening in a loose circle around the open mouth of the police van before she could be fed to it.

Jesus turned to Judas and the others beside them. 'Is there enough of us for me to go?'

Perhaps there were nods, but Judas could only muster a dry-mouthed stare. Simon and Jesus ran to strengthen the circle. Judas relinked with Peter, who was shaking. He missed the warm shelter of Jesus' body.

More police piled on the circle around the van, pulling apart the thread until it split. A red-faced cop pushed several protesters into the ground, forcing the woman into the van.

Through a gap in the crowd, Judas saw Jesus lie down in front of the van as the engine revved. His head was beside the wheel. It would be crushed if it moved. Judas could not see Jesus' face. If the van rolled over anyone's head, Judas wanted it to be his. And he wanted Jesus to see it happen, and to know he had done it for him.

'You're under arrest,' a cop said, cuffs in his hand. 'Do you hear me? You're under arrest.' He stood on Jesus' hand in his regulation boot.

Judas broke loose from the picket. 'Judas!' Peter called, but it was too late. He ran like a dog slipping a lease.

A cop was dragging Jesus up. Judas tackled the cop with his skinny wire of a body. The ridges of the bulletproof vest felt like cartoon abs against his stomach; the ham fist rose up and splintered the fine bones of his nose.

Jesus—forehead cracked with fresh blood—pulled Judas away, hauling him close and linking their arms, beckoning the person closest to him to link, pushing the cops back.

'No one left behind!' Jesus shouted. 'No one left behind!' He was alive with fury, blood on his surgical blue mask, hair frayed.

A many-mouthed snake they circled the van again, pushing relentlessly at the cops who were pressing in. They expanded and, unwillingly, Judas let go of Jesus. On the other side of the van, he caught sight of Peter and Matty: the picket line had dissolved entirely now. Peter's eyes were chlorine blue, his mask expanding and deflating as he breathed harshly. Matty gave a wiggle of his eyebrows above his pink mask, as if to say to Judas, *Crazy, right?*

Judas felt snotty blood drip down the back of his throat. It was hard to believe what was happening. Deep down, Judas had not truly believed the state would fail him. Sure, ACAB and all that—but come on, it's not like we're in America.

'Why are you targeting us?' a cop spat at Jesus. 'Come here for your cause, that's fine. But what do we have to do with it?'

There was nothing Hollywood about them, Judas thought. Oh, how he longed to spit his blood on the cold concrete floor and say, *Is that all you've got? You'll have to kill me.*

'Fuck you!' Judas spat. 'All cops are bastards!'

If he was honest with himself (and he wasn't honest often, thank god, or there would be no story, no Jesus and certainly no gospel) it was a relief to now have the lived experience to echo these sentiments with honest conviction. Like, yeah! Fuck the police! They kicked my crush in the stomach! They stood on his beautiful hand!

The managers were now watching from the window of reception. Judas was being pressed from both sides; the air squeezed out of him. One cop reached for his baton, and then they all did.

Everything became fragmented and swept away. A wave of police violence was unleashed: more were pushed to the ground, some kicked while they were down there. Others were punched or pepper sprayed. Judas was hurt himself, though later wouldn't remember it happening. The van drove away, the woman inside.

The horses charged, their riders towering over the crowd. The plastic over their eyes gave the horses a flat, toy-like appearance, but Judas could smell their sweat, feel the heat of their hot, unwieldy bodies.

One, a grey, reared up over the crowd, and the officer riding it fell to the ground. Hooves were sharp—at school, Judas had known a horse girl with a crescent moon scar on her cheek—so he ran. They all did, pushed to where more vans waited to arrest them.

Except Jesus, and Judas who stopped to watch him. Jesus held out his hand for the horse to smell. He patted her on the muscled neck and said, whoa, girl, whoa. His hands were well-used. Judas would bet that they rasped like denim.

Jesus turned back to Judas. The horses' reins were in his hand, though Judas hadn't seen him take them.

'Can you ride her?' Jesus said.

Inwardly, Judas stared open-mouthed. Can I what her?

Outwardly, Judas stared closed-mouthed.

'Uh huh,' he said, yeah, naturally…

Before he could think, he had one foot in the stirrup and was climbing on top of the animal. Jesus' warm hand was in Judas', pulled to ride behind him; whether his hand rasped, Judas forgot to note, distracted by the soft electricity dance of his skin on his skin on his skin.

The images went viral, of course. Judas became the radical queer cowboy of Glasgow for a time. Jesus escaped death. They thought, for a bit, that they might win. Haven't you ever been in love?

Colin Herd

Birthday Kale

I visited a temple—ran a long way to get there
and couldn't get in. Couldn't sleep because
I'd been reading about Historical Jesus and his
teddy bears all night
Historical Jesus:
you are very sweet like a little cake
and now I will design one with you in
mind I think strawberries the colour of sunburn
banana chips edible grass green tea flavour
a thick moussey custard something whipped
Would Historical Jesus like sprinkles?
oh yes yes Historical Jesus is vegan
we know already
all the creamy stuff is non-dairy
for Historical Jesus's delectation
historical Jesus shuns the Ketos
and the sugar fascists
and the carb avoiders
historical Jesus likes Capybaras and Otters equally
historical Jesus talks a good game
licks the yoghurt lid of life
and also Historical Jesus has very low ebbs
and there are articles about historical Jesus

and testosterone in the context of mental health
I went in a cafe and left without ordering anything
but I want everyone to know that I tried
I read some stories
Historical Jesus's opinion on nutrition is
as valuable as anyone else's
Stop trying to help me I say to historical Jesus
Let me make my own mistake(s)
about pavements and why they're made from
what they're not actually made from
I said to historical Jesus
the last thing anybody needs
is a messiah complex as a birthday gift

Colin Herd

Pulled Teeth

very pleased to write these tongue twisters
that's gonna be a bee or
the amount of typos made me think
have you watched prison break
read Lauren Groff's novel *Matrix*
link and switch link and switch
a pain au
you know a flipping hautboy
is a form of oboe?
in the vicinity of
Polmont which you called Lolmont
said
I'll close the Sun roof
you said it's flawless
in case of dog shit
guy in smug gives me
staff discount every time I buy
a coffee which is minimum once
per day
in the sunshine
in the rain whatever the weather I have
no particular clue what *Lilo & Stitch* is
today I'm reading about spirituality

spirituality gives me the heebee jeebies
but I'm not averse to
my Spanish teacher asked
which epistolary novels in particular
me gusta
and my mind went blank
'cept *I Love Dick*
I ran slower today than
a week ago and I can't
explain why so much
hablame en español o no me hables
they were deliberate and I started
to see only them
said 'this is the smile
I like, the strong tail that
whips me and cute'
and well yeah ok
my smile has something guess
especially in a cap
all my jokes are meaningless
and my poems
which I didn't even imagine
mean
practically zilch
in comparison
to yours

Colin Herd

Fizzy Peach

there's a kind of peach
called cling
what's your ideal
love of your life
this was my sports
massage therapist
when you can speak
she added real or
cake I said
relapsed into my poem
drumming up disinterest
like normal, normal, normal, normal,
sorry whaaaaaaaaat
you sent me three
pics of a red SEAT
no caption and when
I said 'looks good'
you just thumbs-upped me
as a kid and I was born in 1985 I dreamed
of Siri taking me out on a date
we went to a washing machine
factory and the attendant
checked our rucksacks and pencil cases

saying 'just in case you're smuggling
in a landlord!'
I was like I can see them I can see them
and she was like you cannot
the existence of
flumps
got told this joke about the
contents of a lasagne haha
you think a watch'll be hidden in
there in amongst the
whatever ingredient
it's made with
got sheets of paper everywhere
after the lecture I called my mum and cried
two people were down on modern art and I was
afraid to ask what everyone else thought
or even what modern art meant, by them
Joan of Arc Joan Mitchell Joan from the chapel
at work just three cool Joans I like a lot
I also like the person in the
cafe bar for postgrads but I don't know their
name they always say 'hi colin!!!!!!'
that's literally all it takes for my
affection some people are
like living and dying are the same
thing and I'm like no you're mistaken
i had a long very involved
dream about my gran going missing
as we crossed the road in Linlithgow
and then I had to have a pavement
supervision with someone who

looked blankly at me whenever I suggested
they send me some work and eventually
I lost my temper and said work is a
euphemism for poetry send me some
poetry that's all you have to do now let
me look for my gran inside the cafe i
went to check if she was there
and someone with a chaired professorship
someone from my dept
is that the right term was offering
Tea around and there was just enough
room for my butt on the bench so i
briefly sat down and then someone
said 'this is a squeeze' so I got up
i never found my gran in the dream
really I became familiar with the
feeling of searching
kids sandwiches are just as good
as the real thing
I was going to do a coffee order
but got invested in the
wiki of the sugar glider

Shona Floate

GIRLFRIEND

do you pluck her viscous
heart strings
even when she exhausts you ?

she resides in the crook of your elbow
languid and odd
until the girls come and shelve her

out of sight she knows that she
is potent like
she can't be in your arms

pour a pint and she'll confess
to having been a martyr
chop her up like st. serapion
and love her lonely parts

Shona Floate

~

i think i'm the moon
and i think i can see myself
reflected in your eyes

o i'm cold and lofty
until you push your chic red
fingernails into me

and my skin splits like a
watermelon my watery
entrails slide towards you

across the vinyl tabletop
making rafts out of sugar
packets we need a waitress

i'm bleeding juice like a
motherfucker there isn't enough
blue roll in the world for

this spillage and you just keep
pushing
and it's not the moon in your eyes

it's a lighthouse
and you're her mute and lonely
keeper and you reach the

big black seed inside me
you run your thumb along
crack me down the middle

and the stars have jagged edges
and they spill their amber light out

the moths flap towards salvation
and they crash upon the rays

Shona Floate

BEHOLDEN

i'm still learning my sedation
i hold hope under my duvet
suffocating between my thighs
i never felt so alive
i emerge
unvictorious
a poor vessel
more poor than you're used to
i bury coins under the kitchen sink
i hope they appreciate in value
the strange woman in the window
catches me crying
clasps my tears through the glass
and holds them
                            beheld
i am beholden

there's a girl on that moonbeam !
               she's sipping a guinness
i hope that she'll come sip on me
                     when she's finished

Heather Parry

CORDYCEPS

Frances fretted about the bed linen, which seemed now old and frayed. Frances fretted about the bed linen, and then told herself to stop; it was silly, to worry about such a thing, when the girl would barely notice. The girl would be lost in grief. Frances must tiptoe around her, not intruding, bringing meals to her door and running her baths and ironing the clothes she might extricate from the girl's rucksack. Would the spare room be too barren? She pulled a string of spider's web from the headboard; Frances did not often have guests. Perhaps the girl would prefer Frances's bed, as it was slightly bigger and the mattress less firm, the covers marginally softer than the ones on the spare bed, which struck Frances now as selfish and indulgent.

The girl, Delia, arrived late, as the flight was delayed, and then there was traffic from Heathrow, and the drive was long anyway; so gabbled the cab driver, a soft-faced man who had the haunted look of someone who'd been witness to suffering. She must have cried the whole way, for now she was red-eyed and dry, her face slick with recycled air. Frances envied those who could weep stoically, attractive tears falling down their faces in cinematic scope, their sorrow only serving to highlight the unsullied sweep of a cheek, the high angle of a cheekbone, a strong jaw from which a tear might drop.

The dead-eyed Delia swept a blond wave behind her ear and Frances thought: *what it must be like to be so easily beautiful.*

Frances paid the driver without interjection from Delia, and Delia chose the guest room, though Frances offered her own room several times; as she looked into it, it appeared miserly, with its two thin pillows and sun-aged quilt. Very little passed between the two women; there was no hug, for which Frances was grateful. Delia mumbled something about tiredness and retreated immediately to her room. Frances stayed up til the early hours, listening for any movement to suggest an untended-to need. There was no sound but for a quiet sobbing and a scattered, torn snoring, the sort that a lover would find charming.

It was a surprise when Delia presented herself for breakfast, and Frances was glad she'd set the table just in case; there were cereals and Welsh cakes and a mound of fresh fruit, but the younger woman reached for a slice of toast and a cut of butter. Frances wished she'd gone to the farm shop nearby, for their home-churned butter with the thick specks of salt. It was only when Frances poured tea into Delia's cup, pushing the small jug of milk in her direction, that the girl engaged with the fact of the moment: in this house, with this stranger, eating a lukewarm slice of toast.

'This is a lovely place you've got,' said Delia, flatly, with much effort. 'You don't get houses like this nowadays.'

'Yes, I suppose I'm very lucky,' said Frances, immediately riven with guilt. The cottage was solid and well-kept; not enormous but certainly too big for a single woman. And she had got it for nothing, had simply moved into it after university, one of the houses long passed down through her family, which now, in the presence of Delia, this young woman, seemed unutterably obscene.

'It technically belongs to my parents, of course.'

What she meant to say, was trying to say, was that she didn't own it, and she intended that as a negative, an attempt to prove that they weren't so different from one another. But of course they were, and it was bad enough that she hadn't had to buy it, and had never given a penny in rent. She stared into her tea but could feel Delia take her in for the first time, this woman so much older than her, cloistered in a house filled with things she had never paid for, and she could almost hear the thought: *how can* your *parents still be alive?*

Delia looked at her searchingly, then disappeared again into her toast. She looked younger than her twenty years, collapsing into the dining room chair. Wherever she had been doing her field studies, the weather had given her a deep colour, had streaked white in her already pale hair. Holding the bread listlessly as she chewed, she might even be a child. Frances wished she knew something about the girl, wished she'd kept up the letters to Delia's mother, worked through the awkwardness, through her jealousy as the other woman flew abroad, left their little laboratory, left her. Flourished.

'My father will be here in a few days,' Delia said, without taking her eyes off the grain of the table's wood. 'He's got to wrap things up with his other family then he'll be here to get me. Help me with all the paperwork and stuff.'

Frances could think of nothing to say. She had never had to deal with death, not the minutiae of it. It had only encroached on her life in vague and barely affecting ways; a great aunt, over a hundred, leaving a packet of money; the family dog, never to be replaced; the indistinct sadness of other people, failing to reach out of the periphery of her life. Even this death occurred to someone she had long ceased to know, a person for whom she had grieved differently, many years before. She sat in the awkwardness, let herself be consumed by it: it was a penance, she thought, for how everything had become so jumbled. For how she had managed to get so far in life with such little suffering, when others had their lives crumble so young, the movie-star years of their life fractured and turned into something so much heavier.

A few days passed, and no father appeared. Frances felt they'd fallen into a gentle enough pattern, with their quiet breakfasts and Delia's tears echoing across the afternoon, though the small patch of eczema on Frances' right palm had been scratched to flakes and she often felt claustrophobic, as if the walls she knew so well were pulling inwards, the air of the house growing thicker. She began to take her afternoon tea in the garden, where there was more space to breathe; where there was quiet.

A week after the girl had arrived, she spent the evening escalating her agony, weeping with such increasing severity that by midnight she was screeching, the very sound of it painful, her desperate coughing afterwards suggesting that she could barely contain it, could barely get enough oxygen. Frances stood by the spare room, one palm against the handle and one against the door, for over an hour; the girl was suffering, and needed someone. She needed to be held, to be told it was okay to feel these terrible things. But Frances could not enter the room; she could not explain it, but she felt at her core that this girl did not belong to the same world as her. As the hallway grew hot and tilted on its axis Frances realised she was not breathing, and as she got to the floor, the door at her back, her legs bent, the sound from inside the room stopped. Over the rest of the night there was little noise, but for the pages of books being turned, the rattle of drawers being opened. As the day broke, Frances ran herself a bath and tried to imagine she was in the house alone once more.

At the table the next morning the girl was renewed. She asked for peanut butter, of which Frances had none, and coffee, which was consumed with a nose wrinkle suggesting it was below the standard expected; Frances did not drink it, and had picked the most expensive from the supermarket shelf, but realised now there must be a specialist shop, and cursed herself for not having asked. Delia was lively, almost unsettlingly so, and Frances wondered for a moment if she might be in the grips of some illness, perhaps having taken in a parasite from dirty water, as one often will have brief periods of positive energy and even hilarity before becoming gravely sick. Between mouthfuls, Delia began to speak about the research she'd been undertaking, about what had taken her so far—Brazil—in the first place: a location-specific fungi that overwhelmed an insect's system and took it over from the inside.

'You studied fungus too, right?'

Frances shook her head too briskly, as if trying to rid her hair of a fallen leaf. She never imagined the girl would have heard about her life.

'No,' she said, eventually. 'No, that was what your mother did afterwards. At the university we studied yeasts.'

The girl waited, wanting specifics, but Frances had become so used to protecting the details of her life that she found herself unable to say anything more. Delia reached further still.

'And then you left academia?'

Frances nodded, though this was not the case; she had simply shifted from research into a background role. She wondered at the visibility of her life on the internet, how successful she had really been at keeping herself hidden. The girl must have gleaned all this from the university's webpages, looking her up on airport WiFi. Or had her mother spoken about her after all, about her disappointment when she left the lab and Frances had given up on everything they'd worked for?

'My father is going to be delayed,' said Delia quickly, looking directly into Frances' eyes. 'A family emergency or something. He says he'll be here as soon as he can. Could we turn up the heating, and maybe open the blinds?' She smiled sweetly, reaching for another slice of toast and knocking a half cup of black coffee across the tablecloth. 'I'm used to a different climate.'

There was no more wailing, though Delia still kept to her room, and twice asked for the heating to be turned up further, which Frances did, though she found it stifling. In the afternoon Delia appeared, to ask if she might use the washing machine, and Frances fluttered around her, saying she would do it, she wouldn't hear of it, it was the least she could do. So Delia left her still-damp rucksack outside her door and Frances laundered the contents, shaking dead mini beasts from the folds of shirts, brushing mud from sock wool and bleaching the hint of green mould from a towel. She had once done this for the girl's mother, in this same laundry room. When she unfurled the sleeping bag, she found that it was infested, or rather colonised, with a white matter; not mould, for it didn't slide away beneath the finger, nor powder, for it wouldn't be blown. This web of microfingers stretched across the material, stiff yet yielding, unwilling to let go. Frances hung the bag, unwashed, in the laundry room, thinking that some air might soften the web, but when she came in to attend to the dryer later she found the atmosphere heavy with a kind of dust, and with her hand over her mouth she took the sleeping bag from the room and out into the garden, where she stamped on it uselessly, as if it were alive. With a tea towel over her face she unzipped the bag and opened it up, and there she found two dozen bouquets of the most beautiful mushrooms, tall and pale yellow; thin stemmed with a neat rounded top. She reached out to pick one, getting low to the ground and peering deeply into the blossom's fleshy gills, which were scattered with dew and, she found, wet beneath her fingers. It was intoxicating. But as the light in the sky shifted, Frances saw the cloud of breathy spores in a shaft of sun, and with this she grabbed the hose, drenching the bag, and stamping the mushrooms into the ground with her bare feet.

At breakfast, Delia was engaged in a way Frances had not yet seen. She even offered to make the tea, and Frances accepted, for she thought she might be coming down with a cold; the inside of her nose had tickled for hours, and her breathing was slightly laboured. She turned down Delia's offer of toast, and instead stirred thick honey into her teacup, hoping it might work against the dry scratch of her throat. When Delia suggested she might walk into the village later, to buy some warmer jumpers and replace some items she had left in the rainforest, Frances found herself nodding, though the roads were country lanes without a hint of pavement, and the girl might find herself run down by a local or having to escape into a bull's field if she wasn't careful. The village would not take well to an overfamiliar stranger, but she couldn't say these things, and so simply agreed. By the time Delia left the house Frances was already running a bath, as she was chilly despite the quite ludicrous heat, and she drained the tub and refilled it twice with new warmth before she heard the girl return. She stayed in the bath for another full hour, and as she dried herself she saw in the mirror a pale blossom beneath the skin on her shoulder; a cloudy plume, like white ink dropped in water. She would have to take herself to the pharmacy; it must be her age.

At the following day's breakfast Frances was lethargic, drained by a restless night shivering in the relentless heat and exhausted by Delia's fevered questioning. How many people lived in the village? Did she know people well? What was her schedule with regards to her parents, her responsibilities, the things that were expected of her? Frances thought how like her mother she was, in this mood; effervescent, stimulating, overwhelming. Her mother, too, had wanted to know everything about the life Frances had there, in that little cottage, and the life she might have there, with Frances, and though Frances had at first been energised, and played along, and even encouraged her, when she woke up on that second day of their single weekend together the air had felt suffocating, and the cottage too small, and she thought of the way that the residents of the village would forever look, with their dark little eyes, so much like hers, how she would never again have anything like anonymity, how she would always be that woman, in that cottage, living that kind of existence.

Frances took to the bath again, running it hot again despite the fact the air was too saturated with heat, and struggled down into her lungs, which felt tight. She slept, and woke, and as she hauled herself out of the bath, panting heavily, she looked into her mirror and saw that the white inkstain had bloomed across her stomach and onto her breasts.

Nights passed, and Frances slept long, fevered, broken sleeps. Against Delia's entreaties she dragged herself to the kitchen each day. There, Delia made the tea, and buttered Frances' toast, and held it to her lips; it would be okay, she would look after everything, she would make everything in here just like new. One afternoon, she covered the sweating Frances in a blanket, slipping an arm round a shoulder to help her to the guest bedroom, and Frances found herself agreeing: the girl would look after it all well, this life of hers. She would use it much better than Frances ever had.

As Frances lay on her softened sheets, blanketed by the cloying heat, she could feel the million fingers of the fungus reach across her skin and make its web. It would be a nice existence, here in the spare room, with a youngster about the house. A new life through Delia, with her sun-blanched hair and her brightened cheeks. This girl, braver in who she was, in the things she wanted; who would make the world shape itself around her instead of folding herself into its shadows. As Frances tried to open her mouth and found that she couldn't, the first pale yellow mushroom bloomed from her pale-marked chest. It was beautiful; effortlessly so.

Eve Brandon

THE LAST ARCTIC BIRDS OF THE BRITISH ISLES

Before these long years of apocalypse, of plague and heat and rats, this whole island would have thrummed with bird noise. I miss those calls, each a minor, canonical agony—a moan, a sob, a shout, a wail. I think that the rats must be very hungry by now, with so many birds gone. I hate them, hard enough to make my heart pound. It is with a sick pleasure that I watch you wipe the sweat from your face, crouch in dark earth, and scatter poison where it will best serve. The little pellets of poison are tiny, barely the size of a fingernail. I wonder if you'd like to kill me, mashing them into my porridge, lacing the edges of my pillow, feeding them to me on the tip of your tongue. The first couple of times we did this it felt scientific. Now, watching your silhouette outlined in hazy sunlight, I see you burning and salting the earth, I see you a world-destroyer, apocalypse-bringer, rat-bane, death-dealer. It's not not sexy. Between entering notes into our rodent-killing spreadsheet, I inspect your quick hands.

Things were perfect last night, until you said no.

It is near dark when we are finished, and we march back to the bothy. It's still humid, but getting cold, the sweat icy in the hollows of my clothing. Your knees are stiff, the small of my back aches, our bags are considerably lighter. You make up a saucepan of pallid tea before I have a chance to intervene.

I perch on the dissolving sofa and you curl up upon the air mattress. I cannot see your face, just the frantic glow of the little field laptop around your bowed head. I drink the foul concoction, my hands soaking up the warmth, and listen to the wind slip through the tarp pulled tight across the pockmarked shingles of the roof. I press my hot fingers to the stone behind me, where the wall warps and bulges. My skin comes away smelling sweet, like damp earth. It is a crypt smell, a tomb smell. As I look up into the blue shadows of the ceiling, all I can think about is the ground below.

I wake before you. The air in the bothy is thick and hot with the smell of food and our sweating bodies. My skin feels unhealthily warm and tacky, and pain radiates along the edges of each shoulder blade. You are face down in your travel pillow. I pull on my jumper, damp to the touch, and fumble around in the grey light until I find my wash bag. I manage to clamber outside while you pretend to sleep on.

The warmth of the day hasn't settled, and I look out across the coarse grass to the sea beyond. The light is odd, with dark clouds overhead and glades of clear sunlight gleaming far out across the water. In this strange twilight, the mainland is just a smudge across the horizon. I think, for a moment, that I see the distant, graceful turn of one of the many wind turbines they dug into peatland to build, but it is gone before I am sure, and I cannot find it again. I imagine being stuck here forever with you. I don't think you could dump me if we were the only ones left. I would stay inside all day skinning rats for you, sluicing poison from their guts and pulling silvery bones from their meat. I imagine arraying you in rat pelt, plaiting your hair with blue tarp, pounding soap from ash and fat to keep you warm and clean. I imagine welcoming you home each evening, rat soup hot on the hearth, and sitting together on the sofa to watch the tide come in and in and in. I look at you, and I think of the life we could have, if only the world were ending.

'Nat?' you say. 'Are you alright?'

In the door of the bothy, you are sleep-mussed and swollen. I can spot a slither of sunburnt scalp where your hair parts, and I would do anything to kiss it. Anything except stepping closer to you.

You love me, I know. But not enough for forever.

'Yeah,' I say. You blink at me, expectant. You're breaking my heart. 'Just lots to do.'

You are quiet for one, long moment, as you look beyond me to the creeping tide.

'The water looks rough,' you say softly. 'What time did you say the boat is coming?'

I want to push into the circle of your arms, cup my hands so tight around your face that all you can see is mine. I want to dig my nails in. I want to claw something loose. I want you to tell me that the spark is, in fact, still there. That you still feel the same way about me. That you want to move in with me, actually, even if you have other girls, even if your friends don't like me, even if what we have isn't what you need.

'Early tomorrow,' I say, instead. 'Are you that eager to leave?'

You laugh. I watch your hands flex in and out of fists at your sides.

We eat breakfast as we walk to the northern cliffs and you are only ever one step behind me. I chew my slice of bread—white, unbuttered—until it is a homogenous clot in the depths of one cheek. Above the slow, swollen wind, I hear your hayfeverish wheezes. It became easier and easier, as I got to know you, to imagine you old. I can see where the little hairline cracks will wear into deep wrinkles. I don't look back, but there you are before me.

I am shocked once more by the quiet, as if rats are supposed to die loudly, in a backward cacophony of wing beats and bird song. The wind turns suddenly, carrying a sweet, carrion smell. It glazes my tongue, clings in my throat, catches in the long tendrils of your pale hair. A rat curls, small and dark, in the mouth of a burrow. Saliva pools upon my tongue as nausea builds, and disgust gives way to hunger. In the wet heat the corpse has become riddled with new life. Beneath the soft spill of fur, many unseen things writhe. Distantly, I understand how odd it is, for this to have happened so swiftly.

I think about this barren, sun-bleached island, where nothing will ever be the same again. I want to push you aside, kneel, and dig my fingers into the thin skin of the rat's stomach. I want to pull gouts of fur from its sleek back and peel its skin clean from its shining bones. I prod it with the very tip of my boot, and it splits open, ripe. This rotten crop. This revenant beast.

You retch, and spit loudly onto the stone before you, a long thread of slime dangling from your panting mouth. I remember the first time we kissed in one dark corner of the club. You had tasted of Tequila Rose and watermelon ice vape fluid and I had opened myself to you anyway. You had kissed with your mouth stretched wide, as if you were promising me everything. Wet, and warm, and close.

I put a hand to your back and feel the shifting muscles beneath your T-shirt. We spend some time there, holding vigil for the warfarin-bloated creature. I pretend that we are waiting for the gulls to begin circling, in order to punctuate this long and miserable murder. But the skies are as still and as quiet as ever. I stoop to help you up, bracing my hands beneath your elbows. I end up squatting there for too long, watching the exquisite clench of your jaw. We lurch to our feet together, two halves of one ungainly whole. You lay your temple on my cheek, your breath hot on my throat.

'Tell me it's worth it,' I say into your hair.

You look up, face too close for me to see the full breadth of your expression. When you speak, your voice is slow and soft. Between us, the rat continues to rot, quiet and lush with new life.

'Oh Nat,' you say. 'This won't bring the birds back.'

The rain begins slowly as grey cloud sweeps low across the island. The waves surge upward, white and florid, as they hit the shallower ground of the bay. I feel claustrophobic with my hood up, surrounded by the sound of my own breathing. The wet metal of the zip and my constant, seeking tongue scours my lips red and sore. The storm swells, and breaks. We run back to the bothy, the rain whipping at my face. I am half wild with it, by the thunder of my pulse, the moan of the wind, and the beat of your feet behind me. This is it, I think. I try to look out to the mainland, but I can barely see past the white spray of waves over the shore. This is it, the flood. I imagine a world wiped clean. I am suddenly terrified, as if I hadn't wished for this. I come to a sudden, stumbling stop. You almost fall over me, but I grasp for you. I tear my hood down and try to think of what you want to hear.

'Please,' I shout into the wind. 'I'm sorry. I don't want to fight, I don't want things to change. Don't leave me. I'm happy. I promise, I'm happy.'

A dog at your feet.

You shake your head viciously, but you're already leaning in. There isn't time to process it, just a looming glimpse of your eye, the water on your cheeks and a mouthful of your sodden hair. I take a handful of your raincoat in my fist. I don't let you pull away, just hold your mouth to mine in an uneven clash of teeth. You try to kiss me, and all I can do is think of how lucky I am to have dragged you back, and breathe desperately into your body.

As you push into me, corralling me up the small hill and into the shadow of the bothy, I remember our first time together. You were the first girl I'd ever been with. You weren't so different to a boy, except for how long it took. You look different, smell different, taste different here, at the end of all things. I let you kiss me in a wet trail down my neck before I am pulling you into the bothy and onto the sofa. I slip a hand beneath your shirt and grasp at the pad of fat at your stomach. You're not wearing a bra, and so I can work my fingers up the length of you until I am half caught inside your clothes. I want you to take me inside you, until I am subsumed completely. I want you to eat me up—spread on toast, ground to meal, pickled in brine. Outside the wind howls, and I can hear a great thundering of waves against the rocky shore. I think of all the little rat bodies, shredded by the seething water, washed clean by the salt and cold.

You pull away, the sudden chill making me gasp. I reach for you, desperately, my hands sliding across the slick gooseflesh on your arms. You twist to peel your shirt from your body and throw it into the corner of the room. I see a sliding glimpse of the bones in your back, the stark curve and swell of each rib and vertebrae. You push me down into the wet-dog smell of damp polyester and sofa cushion. Above you, the tarp ripples and warps, sucking and billowing into strange, organic shapes. The constant, static hiss of rain on plastic fills my mind. You fumble between us for my fly, sliding your hand awkwardly between my legs. It can't be comfortable, but I think you're too busy riding my thigh to notice. Your hair falls lank around us and all I can see is the dark well of one pupil. As you shift your fingers against me, the tarp beating like a heart above us, I am struck by a sense of unreality. I do not recognise the odd ways the wavering light stretches your face. The snuffling sound of your urgent breathing through a blocked nose sounds dislocated from you, as if there is an animal at the door. I pull a finger across your wet lips, and stare up into your teeth. I understand you to be a mask over the face of something else. Just beneath your skin, something rotten curls.

It is a revelation, a relief, to know you like this. It all feels so simple. I push gently at the soft space between your hip and rib cage, and feel your body give beneath my fingers. You allow yourself to be rearranged, our legs tangling as you slide down the sofa into the warm space I vacate. I look down at you, and think about our forever. I extricate your body from the rest of your clothes, revealing the fine hairs on your shins, and the acne rashes down the back of your thighs. I cradle each of your heels in my palm, and pull the sodden socks from your shrivelled feet. I settle between your legs, and look down into the red gape of your mouth. I think about spitting down into your gullet, but I don't think you'd let me kiss you again if I did. Your fingers flex against my scalp, pulling me in, and I can hear the rasp of my hair through the bones of my skull. I slide my tongue across the

147

thin, velvet skin on the inside of your arm, as sleek and as supple as down.

I bend further, and place a loose, open-mouth kiss to your sternum. You are making little, half-formed noises as my teeth press into the soft cavity just beneath your ribs. I press my nails into your fraying skin, working my tongue into the wound, and your body sighs open before me. I lick my lips, and you taste like stagnant water, of seaweed, of sulphur. The pink of your insides are filmed with clouds of white salt, the coiled meat of you sticky to the touch. You pet, absently, at the back of my neck. I press closer, and my seeking tongue finds something slick and unyielding. Inside your stomach, as if it has grown like a pearl within you, a single, white egg. I look up the length of your body to find you watching me through half-lidded eyes. Your hand finds my face, touching the tears upon my lashes. You twist your wrist, and take up a handful of my hair. I am pulled into place, head cushioned in the hollow of your hip. Held still by your palm, surrounded by the deep shadows of your body, all I can do is listen to the rush of the tides and the steady rhythm of your breathing.

I sleep fitfully, waking repeatedly to your slight movements. I get up just before dawn to piss. Your face is blueish and gaunt in the thin moonlight. Outside, the wind has ebbed, leaving the night cool and quiet. I squat in the wet grass. All before me is the syrup-dark sea. I cannot imagine the land I know to be on the other side. Just the endless waves and my own shadow, stretching across the grass to meet the coming tide. It is as if I could reach out a finger and touch the darkness. Smear it with a thumb. Lick it from the skin of the world.

I sit on the beach as light slips over the horizon. Some trick of the current has disgorged heaps of debris along this side of the island. I find myself amongst oddly twists of plastic and rope, bleached sweetly pastel by sa. and by sea. Where the tide eases in, I can see the bodies of birds, beading the shoreline. They are miraculously whole, untouched by rats, but ravaged by flu. Beneath the matts of sand and seaweed, their shanks are black with blood, their small heads distended, and their necks twisted to odd angles. This poor, blighted island. These poor, blighted birds.

The morning brightens and the sun shines from some unseen point in the wide expanse of sky, the light blurry and diffused. The sea is perfectly still, stretching silvery into the mist. I watch the boat pull closer, its sleek nose clipping through the water. I am sad, I think, to see it. You'll be lonely here, just you and the rats. I promise to think of you often, and how your bones may see the birds return to this picked-clean place. I pull myself to my feet, each joint clicking. I wonder if I could excavate the abandoned burrows of this island, pull all the little bird bodies from their graves, and press a feather into each of your freckles. I wonder if you'd have let me take your body to the water to scour you clean and perfect. I wonder if we could have been made anew.

Cal Bannerman

LANDSLIDE

1.

The mud woman puts her ear to the earth, which is here peaty and not unlike her own skin. Lichen on a nearby pebble unhooks feathery tendrils from the stone, flakes off like dandruff, begs a favour of the passing breeze and alights on the mud woman's buttocks. There it sunbathes, intrigued by the patterns which leaves and clouds and flitting songbirds score into the afternoon.

2.

If you cut a worm in half, right down the middle where the fingernail-pale tube wraps the body like an Elastoplast™ bandage, it will grow two new sides and two new selves. Children know this implicitly: a sort of inherited understanding of the world or example of convergent evolution wherever earthworms are present. But children are messy and rarely possess the hand-eye coordination for precision surgery. Moreover, it is an urban myth. Grandmother Mud collects the shrivelled and sundried corpses of worms sloppily severed. She brews them into a tea which tastes of beetroot and week-old custard, and serves it at church coffee mornings for £1.50 a cup.

3.

Clouds return drunk from the pub, ruddy cheeked and swollen bladdered and tense. Below them on the flaccid land a woman sculpted of mud strikes the plough pose, *halasana*, and tilts her vulva to the skies. She bares it with crow-bone fingers, banks of soft clay red as rust and seafloor sand. Dislocates her jaw wide as it will go, opens her ears; flares nostrils bubbling sulfuric as geysers. The pressure of waiting gives her a headache. When the rain finally does break, her body becomes a sloughing landslide, a litany of pollinated seeds sensing long-awaited succour. She floods the valley with her sucking earth, killing 19, rendering dozens more homeless.

4.

A photographer trekking in the Shenandoah Valley in search of wild boar snaps a shot of the treeline across the river, rising toothpick straight from a bed of bracken and brush. Only when the celluloid is developed will they notice a brown, bipedal blur marching through the forest. It will not make them rich or famous. Mud haunts the photographer's dreams until, one day, they fill a syringe with slurry and feed it into their veins.

5.

The mud woman goes spelunking once a fortnight. In the deepest caverns she leaves traces of herself. Brackish sediment from the Nile, richly tilled soil from Punjab and wet clumps of alkaline *padi* field; dry Andean clay cracked like eczema upon the earth, and the soft aphrodisiacal stench of freshly dug mud plucked from the hands of a child, digging treasures in their back garden. When the child grows up they will train in geology. The presence in a cave carved during the Pleistocene of samples from a hundred different geographies will put their name on the map. It is the first conclusive evidence of Pangea, even though it is not.

6.

Following the child's fall from grace, as chronicled in a *National Geographic* splash feature, their fortunes continue on a downward spiral. They plant their mother beneath the earth like a rhizome. She always loved nature; she showed the child it was their whole reason for being. Now, the Lady of the Muds spoons and caresses her corpse, weaves maggots into her hair like cowrie-braided dreadlocks, acupunctures her moulting flesh with newborn blades of grass—turns her into a football pitch for ants—pierces her ears again with loose bits of gravel (her lobes closed decades ago), returns her to a foetal position, caulks her body with chalk, takes her toe bones as souvenirs.

7.

To the wolf whistle soundtrack of a peacocking nuthatch, the mud woman whittles nine-sided dice with runes instead of numbers. The runes all mean the same: bog, fen, marsh, mire, moor, quag, swale, muskeg, mud.

8.

Old Mother Mucky Pup arrests houseplant development or sups the overwatering from pots like venom from snake teeth. Old Mother Mucky Pup grows in ominous clumps of hairy black on bathroom grouting, and in long-necked mycelial fronds where kitchen tiling ends and skirting begins.

Old Mother Mucky Pup is lint and dust and the occasional dandelion seed blown in through the open window of a grown boy's living room; she is responsible for the tobacco he smokes and she is the shit building inside him. Old Mother Mucky Pup disdains the indoors: back in her day there were no doors nor walls nor ceilings cement brick mortar electrical wiring toasters kettles toilets nor PlayStation® 5s; but she pushes her way in all the same, just to remind them.

9.

The grown boy grinds, rolls, inhales the mud woman. He is, in fact, a they, and she more like an it. In their lungs it starts to work.

10.

In the stuttering quiet of dawn's dawning, when the moon is at its most menacing and all the birds snooze their alarm clocks, mud woman glistens with frost. Her body is sharp, angular, her shoulder blades carved by glaciers in her salad days, long before she bore lettuce. Under the milk light of that pock-marked satellite she is rigour, she is poise, she is delicate and diamond-hard. Mud woman radiates like the sea at high noon, pulling sailors to their doom, and now she has an idea.

11.

'Charlie! What have I told you about tracking mud into this house!'

'Eugh, this coffee actu'lly pure tastes lit mud. Mingin', man.'

'The earth, that is nature's mother, is her tomb.' [*Romeo and Juliet*, 1597.]

'Jaaack, let's go make mud castles in the garden, c'moooan!'

'Godfather of Chicaga blues, eh? Only t'ing I don't unnerstan' is why he calls hisself Muddy!'

'And as you can see by the stratification of seeds in this fossilised mud, the ancient Iraqis were among the first humans to develop agriculture.'

'Common as muck, that boy.'

'After [Jesus] said these things He spit on the ground, made some mud from the saliva, and spread the mud on his eyes... So again the Pharisees asked him how he received his sight. "He put mud on my eyes," he told them. "I washed and I can see."' [*Book of John*, 9:6-15.]

'It'll be looonelyyy this Christmas...'

'Matthew McConaughey gives the best performance of his career.' [*Cannes 2012: Mud* review, Jason Solomons, *The Guardian*.]

'Don't fuckin' touch me, Alasdair. Why ye aw covered in mud, onywey? Ye look like ye've fuckin' shat yersel.'

12.

The transformation of (they/them) starts slowly, later in life, years after they inhale the mud woman; decades after she makes and then breaks their career. (They/them) is out walking one evening beneath a coppice of stars, an oasis amid dunes of stratus. The field is an oil spill of slick, post-storm earth newly-ploughed; it is a gravitational well clawing at their wellies, hungering to part (they/them) from their artificial soles. A quickening in the blood, a caught breath, a succession of primal shivers invigorating the nervous system; the dusk is empty and full of voice: *slup, slup, sluuup.* They pause, stoop, pinch a fingerful of mud, bring it to their nose and huff. Their thoughts go like this: 'worm, saliva, rugby, Easter, scabby knees, rim job, grubby nails, harvest crop, double, double, soil and rubble, school changing-room showers, hunger, hunger, hunger and womb; she is the earth bookending us.' They paint a moustache in mud upon their upper lip. A really good one. A great big Field Marshal Horatio Herbert Kitchener, 1st Earl Kitchener, KG, KP, GCB, OM, GCSI, GCMG, GCIE, PC-type moustache. 'My country needs me!' they speak to the wind, and step from their wellingtons into the quicksoil. They are knee deep before their senses return.

13.

The muddy maiden is left to dry so she can be better brushed off once-white T-shirts. The muddy maiden is shorn from studded boots logger-sawed between the bristles of a brush station post-match, she is tugged in clumps from the hair of wayfaring toddlers. The muddy maiden collects the arseprints of every stranger compelled by spring heat and summer sun to plonk their derrière upon a dewy hillside. The muddy maiden escapes capture, hidden in the gills of a chestnut mushroom prepped by a line cook who was never taught to brush fungi. Pubescent boys dubbed soldiers conduct slapdash scarification rituals on Our Muddy Maiden with field-issue trench shovels; for four years they dig these graves and die in them; she remembers too vividly the peeling horror for four hundred centuries and more. The muddy maiden is trampled, hewn, baked, spat on, rolled in, watered down, dried out, turned over, fertilised, exhausted, fertilised, exhausted, exhausted, exhausted, exhausted; she is at her wits end, until (they/them).

14.

Their friends start complaining, in secret, that everything (they/them) cooks tastes altogether too earthy. Neighbours notice the russet footprints leading to their flat, the irony smell from beyond the letterbox; they notice, too, the new name gracing flat 2/1's street-level buzzer. A social worker is called to check upon their children, but when she arrives at the flat she finds no evidence of there ever having been any: all the walls are painted brown, the shag carpet brown too, and the tea (they/them) makes her has so little milk it is a similar shade; brown is the colour of divorcee depression, and though the other parent's name on the social care report is unintelligible to her, she's confident the children must be living somewhere else, safe with this so-called 'Mucky Pup'.

15.

When (they/them) stop showing up to work, citing 'the stifling cleanliness of late-stage capitalism and the systemic inability of modern workplaces to satiate Homo sapiens' primordial need for expansive landscapes', the board of directors is suddenly and simultaneously struck by the urge to dump every stock and share they own in Shell, Saudi Aramco, PetroChina, bp, Chevron, SINOPEC, ExxonMobil, LUKOIL, equinor, DUKE ENERGY, ENBRIDGE, NOVATEK and TotalEnergies. Their hedge fund managers don't even query the decisions, having rendered themselves Zen in the mud baths of local spas over the weekend. Global investments in non-renewable energies are shifted overnight to wind farm land-purchasing initiatives and photovoltaic battery storage R&D. Down at the post office, (they/them) seals soil samples inside a Jiffy® *green* eco-friendly padded envelope; they mail it, via paddle boat, to,

Mx Netflix
Netflix HQ
1 Netflix Way
USA, NFX 666

They prepare similar packages for the CEOs of TikTok, X, Meta, Amazon, and Disney. Within a week, #mud is the one and only trending hashtag. The Mud Challenge goes viral, then bacterial, until everyone just stops caring. Content becomes lost in a sea of soil. Soon it dries up completely. Consumers push mud into their headphone jacks and charging ports, wipe mud across their phone cameras, remember what it was to be more than purchasing power. When it rains they walk outside and breathe deeply the lapping tide of earth, bury their devices in the mud, make potions of rose petals and juniper berries, go roly-polying down muddy knolls, unearth treasures of mid-century crockery, ha'penny pieces, rabbit femurs and sword hilts with their mothers' garden trowels, push their fingers to the knuckles in stinking fragrant aromatic mud just to consider its coolness, its dampness, all its squirming life and there—plugged into the earth—they realise.

16.

The mud woman is more than mud, she is shale and brimstone, magma and bog, sub-Saharan and Antarctician, she is life and she is _____. Mud woman is genderless sex. Mud woman is quivering blóð. Mud woman is 47% oxygen, 28% silicon, 8.1% aluminium, 5% iron, 3.6% calcium, 2.8% sodium, 2.6% potassium, 2.1% magnesium, and 100% mud.

17.

Rain falls and turns everything to mud.

18.

As the atmosphere gradually heals, and earth gradually cools, the mud woman closes her eyes. She has been unable to rest for millennia. Sun breaks, a bridge of fantastical colour stitches sky to earth. A once-lauded geologist takes off their skin, reveals their meat is pan-browned mince.

19.

The mud they/them puts their ear to the earth. They have known its song all along.

Jane Flett

BENEDICTION FOR THE GIRLS WHO WANT TOO MUCH

Bless you for your greed hungry girl
who was christened Too Much & instructed
to scythe herself smaller. Bless you for grabbing
hands & the growl of your guts. Bless you
walk into a room needs first demanding
all you desire. Unsure the world
will provide but agape anyway & waiting
to be delivered or denied. It takes
pluck to show up with flaunted want
while the rest disguise their appetites.
It takes a girl unashamed to reveal all
a girl can crave. The world is full of cowards
who hide the hulk of their proclivity
& then there is you. You, pretty creature
with your heart's doors propped open.
You, rabid heart full of the world.
Life, messily, all over the daylight hours.

Fraser Currie

WHEN PEARL'S LAST UN-INSIDES OILED

elegy for SOPHIE, after Walt Whitman

It's Okay To Cry
when Pearl's last un-insides oiled
& Athens took another slippery blow on its red white
magazines mourned mechanical teardrops with ever-turning clicks

ever-turning clicks, they turned FORM quick to bring
Pearl's oiled synth & slipping blow on the red white
& thought of FORM we shed

Ponyboy
O   O   OH   UH   M   OO   N !
O   **A** CRO **PO** L **CRY** IS **PHAL** MOON !
O   **HYP** **E** O **R** CHEMA **POP** GAZ I MOON!
O CRUELCLUTCHHANDS O OIL ED MOON !
O   VIR GO MOON TEXT URED MOO   N !

Faceshopping
in the face of formless markets
FORM's face markets a warbling form

solo the artist

stylite visionary, propelling alloy palette

paints no form a song

aortic percussion

drums out fettered now (dear FORM we know

if your heart didn't pump you'd waste by living)

Is It Cold In The Water?

cold circle forms ignite the Aegean warm enough

now we know that FORM's water is transcending cold to
swim

as we swam in the solitude the communal warehouse night

as we saw FORM had sound to exceed as FORM scratched
to us night after night

as dopamine bloomed late down & out as if outside (while
the bodies pulled their press)

as MDMA fused our central nervous systems (we sought
hallucinsomnia)

as the bag depleted but FORM's music defeated the dawn
we could not be contained

as FORM melded with Immaterial's decadence & the kindness
of drag queens

as we watched twinks pass out lost to the colourless stage

as FORM's question in its answer happily floated, as where
cold circle forms ignite

finished   bead in the night   & was warm in the water

Infatuation

can we autotune a lament for FORM now formless?
is the reverb enough is the venue enough are we queer enough?
in devotion should sweat be more sincere than scents accented?
see FORM is back(drop) the sea   see the drop
susurrus musk for us sea the smell of abundant leg a sea /
      see coast to coast
frantic popper & snort breeze of close friends corporeal
we'll spray the dancefloor with deconstructions of love

Not Okay

scream IN THE SONIC splutter ING
destroyer: bash & tend to conventional notes, I hear you create
we hear   listen   understand
(react)   (wait our turn)   (more listened / less known)
bodies respond to the tangle but it's just the solipsist & the
      disco ball
disco ball spinning communists & queers into practical
      theories

Pretending

(cellophane void)body/soul   eclipse land
FORM's Glasgow with fig trees & alternating monk / alien
      banshee chants
the melting & the modern amphitheatre, compass of intent,
    Athens's mopeds
      revving engine
traditional Doric columns keeping out plastic moss & porn
lacquer the sun's phallic ray gun

the morning's light bodily fluid
permeable as the production of freedom
the gift of not pretending that we take from thumping aurora
comedown suspicious   unwelcome   exit stairs
over FORM's city shines safety, wrapping man/woman/other

Immaterial
SING   SEQUENCE   SING form's WAVE
CHOP   VOCALS/MATERIAL/CULTURE
     RECORD THE LEAVES
SING   SEQUENCE   SING form's
     INFINITE WAVES

sing boysgirlsbeings, dance beyond prescription
dance bionic simulation, freer than stifling bombs

O   liquid   metal   amalgamate
boysgirlsbeings of FORM'S soul—sing together
we speak only FORM—dark holds us

                                        will soon tempt us
but nownownow   FORM holds us

Whole New World/Pretend World
i.
FORM'S visions pass us in an alcove, a Piranesi strobe
visions see six friends through six grams of separation
passing the flash of the phototropic pheromones
encore, night's dead song, ten minutes long
                    VISIONS

of FORM departing in a pilgrimage to the nebula, tickling
    the ether
              VISIONS
of us, of me and   of you and   we and   of utopia
FORM waves goodbye, subverts the royal primogeniture
we leave memory there in the misfitting, reclaiming the new
    DJ thing

ii.
we weren't pretending   FORM's night was ending
song surpasses melody   mantra of new forms found
        the universe is not too trite to echo profundity
or performance   we perform   the sky & the ceiling of
    repatriated prisons
      we hold hands   boys hold hands   girls hold hands
    they hold hands
we should mobilise   memory our manifesto
    FORM's end the fertiliser
we could be sweeter   than interpolated sugar
    for FORM's sake
twine new tracks with the prism of the present
choose each other under a garish bus light   home.

Samuel Goldie

ONE NIGHT IN BARCA

Ah um stood in ma hostel dorm; chin restin oan ma bunk bed n heid between the space where the railins dip tae make way fur the ladder. Ah huv made room oan ma messy sheets, n in front ae me ur two Rizlas torn in half. While shovellin the freshly crushed dust intae one ae the four papers, the door opens n a guy enters. As someone no particularly known for their cat-like reflexes, ah impress masel at the deftness with which ah move tae hide whit am dain.

Wi a shiny black, poker straight mullet cropped at the neck, sharp features n tanned skin lighter where his hair is shaved, ah think this cunt is absolutely stunnin. A rollie is tucked behind one ae his ears. This is how folk sportin the mullet trend back hame should wish they look.

The guy laughs. There's no need to hide, dude. I'm doing exactly the same. He produces fae his pocket a small clear plastic bag filled wi broon rocks, smilin tae reveal a row ae startlingly white, yet no perfectly aligned, teeth. This makes him aw the mair endearin tae me.

I'm Gabriel, he introduces himself in an accent ah cannae quite place. It's American wi a dash ae suhin else.

Ah accept his ootstretched hand eagerly. Ahm Stephen, ah respond. But maist folk just call me Steg.

Steg… he ponders, pensively, as if it were the maist pressin issue in the world. Yeah, yeah! he nods his heid n points at me, wagglin his index finger. I like that. Never heard it before, that's for sure.

That's cause it's a Scottish hing. Ah suppose that ah, masel, am a Scottish hing in general, if ye couldnae tell by ma accent.

I like you, Steg. He laughs once more; an irresistible sound that moves through the sweaty air between us.

Ah grin lit there's nae the morra. Eh… Aye, aye, ah like you tae—it's been really guid tae meet ye!

He continues, Isn't the guy who vacuums his space at like, six AM, so irritating by the way?

Awwww, mate! ah run ma hands through ma hair n laugh. Whit a fuckin nuisance that cunt is. Ah walked in oan um dain it this mornin. Cunt looked it me lit ah wis a zombie. Then again, ah suppose ah might actually huv looked like one, state ah wis in.

Gabriel laughs once mair. Were you just getting back from the festival?

Aye mate. Class gettin tae explore the city durin the day and then huv that tae attend it night.

My friends and I are going too! Who are you here with?

Just oan ma lonesome, mate. Gives me the freedom tae meet lovely folk like you, unrestricted.

The slightest hint ae a beamer flushes across Gabriel's tanned cheeks. Why don't you come with me tonight, Steg? I'd love to introduce you to my friends, and get to know you a little more myself.

Mate, that wid be class. Ah huv some stuff to sort before ah head in, so why don't ah give you ma number and we cin meet up in the festival itself?

Just as ahm aboot tae get ma phone oot, the door bursts open. A lassie grabs Gabriel by the shooders n says, Emma and Alex are fighting again—

He rolls his eyes, Can't you deal with it? Every single time we're on a trip.

Please, the lassie begs. Alex has just punched a window and it's cracked.

For fuck's sake... Gabriel puts his head in his hands. He looks at me n goes, Can you wait around the hostel for a little while longer? I'll meet you in the lobby once I've dealt with this.

Aye, eh, nae worries. Ah'll either be in here or doonstairs.

Gabriel exits and the dorm is silent again. *Holy fuck,* grins ricochet aff the four walls ae this cramped room while ah turn n continue tae construct ma bombs ae Mandy.

After waitin aboot fur some time in the hostel dorm while nursing a can ae beer, Gabriel doesnae show face. There's a disheartenin weight in ma belly, but ah huv tae push oan wi ma night. At about four o'clock ah jump oan the Metro n get aff at Llacuna. This part ae the city is mair dilapidated than others ah huv seen in the past couple ae days, wi paint peelin aff the blocked buildins n graffiti litterin the now closed metal shop front shutters, however, Barca's spell retains its potency wi generous, open, tree-lined streets. This is nae High Street in a Scottish town, tae be sure, fillin themselves wi one too many a barber n vape shop, other outlets closin up n fleein as the place cin seem tae alienate itself fae the world oan its doorstep.

The street behind me is where ah need tae be. The guy ahm meetin is spotted standin in one ae the shop fronts, indented in a narrow, peach-painted buildin, shrouded by street art. Vibrant colours, however, dinnae match his mood which surprises me, as ah huv built up an amicable relationship wi this cunt the past cutla days. Here he stands, a tall, English, skin-heided guy wi tears in his eyes.

Ye awright? ah look up at um wi a crease in ma brow.

Um, no, not really mate, if I'm being honest with you.

Whit's up?

I can't handle another fucking... another *fucking* night of this! he exclaims, whole body tensed.

Ah place ma hand oan his shoulder n gie it a gentle squeeze afore he pulls me intae a tight hug, chokin the life oot me. The wet ae tears rub against ma cheek as the guy sobs intae ma shoulder. Finally, he lets me go.

I'm sorry about that, he says. I've kicked the arse out it over the past few days, so I have.

Cin ye no just leave it the night, ma man? Take some time tae yersel.

I can't. I think my boss would kill me.

Ah don't take the time tae ask whether this would be literally, or no.

He continues, Anyway, what was it you wanted again? A gram of ket?

Aye, that's the wan. Complimentary ketamine fur ma Mandy.

Finally, ma accomplice breaks a smile. They are quite the combo. Enjoy yourself tonight, my Scottish mate.

Ma feelins ur mixed as ah leave ma dealer pal. He is the first British person ah've spoken tae aw weekend that doesnae seem happy. Everyone ah've met hus been here tae huv fun, fur an escape, wi happiness behind and in the creases ae their eyes. This guy reminds me ae folk at home, in the pub every Saturday oan the gear, smilin away n chattin shite but they are deid at the bar, lookin fur exhilaration in aw the wrong places.

The guid hing about Barca is, despite the fact ah hud never been before, there's always a wiy tae work oot where yer gawn. The city is bordered at the back by hills and tae the front by the sea. If ye cin see the hills, then ye ken yer place within Barca; yer space within Barca.

Ah could choose tae walk along the waterfront tae reach the Parc del Fòrum, a steel n concrete event groond, where Primavera takes place, but instead ah opt tae work ma way through the pastel-coloured blocks and tree-lined streets. Every so often wi a squawk and a flash ae red, green or yellow, a parrot will boost overheid. It's in these moments that ah feel so lucky tae be among these people and these colours compared tae the drab constraints ae back haim. A genuine vibrancy buzzes aboot this place that moves its way through me like an electric current, a sensation ah huv never felt before. As siesta comes tae an end, bars n restaurants begin tae open their shutters. Fresh n potent scents ae food bein prepared float through the air; ah stand oan the spot n take a deep breath in, allowin Barca itself tae consume ma very being.

Ah arrive at the festival entrance. It's surprisingly easy tae get in tae, especially when ye hink aboot the Fort Knox security at similar events at haim. A bored-lookin security guard barely glances in ma bag. Ah move away fae the queues n turn tae the steep slope at the back ae the festival. It's covered in fake grass n topped by a Hollywood-esque sign, each letter lit up n movin up n doon oan mechanical loop: Primavera Sound.

Ah walk tae the bars right at the top n wait fur a beer. Drink in hand, the sun slides intae golden hour, and in front sprawls the rest ae the festival. Throngs ae people weave between the massive concrete legs which stand as the foundations ae massive solar panels. In front ae thum, the pulse ae music fae the stages thrums through the air. Fae here, ah observe the goins on, glazed in honeyed light. Ah mentally sketch oot ma plan ae action, knowin that soon Lorde will be on.

Wi a sudden pang ae romantic devastation ah realise that somewhere, in the vast abyss ae folk below me, is Gabriel.

Tae combat this, before headin tae any stage, ah boost straight tae the toilets fur ma first bomb ae Mandy. N so ma night truly begins.

Primavera's pissers ur far less vibrant than the rest ae Barca. Horseshoe shaped chunks ae the groond are carved oot tae make way fur the grey plastic portaloos. The interior is hot n humid, so ah make ma work quick. The bombs ae Mandy are concealed within a hidden zip ae ma man bag. Luckily, none huv burst. Ah place one ae the papers oan ma tongue n swallow wi a couple gulps ae tasty Estrella Damm. Ah turn tae leave, n catch masel in the mirror. Ma black, curly hair is covered by a bucket hat; a bucket hat which ah hud been lucky tae find, mind you, as ma heid is so big. Both the gold hoops oan ma ear lobes shine through nicely n ah um wearin a blue T-shirt wi a faint tie dye pattern throughout it. Ah feel smashin, if ah do say so masel. Ah'd like tae hink thit Gabriel wid feel the same.

Ah move away fae the toilets n stand fur a second tae get ma bearins. Fae where ah um stood, ah cin see folk streamin through the entrance. One boy comes intae the festival wearin a T-shirt, shorts n fishnet tights underneath. Once past security, he stops in the middle ae everyone n takes both the shorts and T-shirt off, revealin a full fishnet bodysuit wi only red briefs underneath. Ah um the only one who appears tae be payin him any attention. There is no malice in the air here. Only music, fun n acceptance.

The Mandy in ma stomach makes its grand appearance far quicker than ah wis expectin. Ah cin literally feel the paper burst i

Goodness gracious

Ah stumble as ah feel ahm aboot tae whitey n walk intae a silver metal bench; it carves oot a crescent moon shaped gash in ma shin, the pain ae which pulsates through ma entire body n blood begins tae weep fae it. Tears begin tae well in ma eyes it the intensity ae the pain n ah shift tae the groond.

Someone crouches doon next tae me n wraps their arm aroond ma shooders. Ah turn tae find Gabriel, in a white linen shirt wi the top three buttons undone, rollie still tucked behind his ear. Ah eagerly accept his warm embrace, the aftershave oan his neck fragrant and floral, a summery scent tae be sure. His skin is soft. Despite ma best efforts, ah pop a semi.

Gabriel's lips brush against ma ear as he whispers, Come on, I can help you.

He hoists me up. Ah try n hinge ma hips backward tae obscure whit's hapnin below the waistline, yet this causes further pain tae shoot through ma leg. We walk toward a small patch ae beach left clear fae bar stalls. Gabriel grabs a cutla napkins tae clear away the blood, as well as two more beers.

The white ae the napkin is dyed scarlet as ma blood seeps intae it. Tryin no tae concentrate on this, ah take a deep breath in through the nose n oot through the mooth. Water laps gently against the shore. In the distance twinkle the many lights ae a cruise ship, sailin aff intae the horizon. Ma pupils ur beginnin tae vibrate. The ship becomes a smudge ae yellow light oan the inky blue water. Ah slur ma words, Ye no hink it'sh a bit… eh… mental min how the sea effectively closes aw the cunts oan that ship aff fae the world but they're aw probs huvin a class time regardless?

He hands me the beer n ah take a gulp. Ah notice his pupils ur lit flyin saucers. There must be so many of them here, and on the ship, he says quietly. There's tears in his eyes. So many people, all looking for the same.

N whit's that? ah ask, puttin ma arm roond his shoulder.

He wipes at his eyes n goes, I've seen a lot of the world, Steg, I spent the most time during my youth at an international academy in the Caribbean—you can probably tell by my accent. But no place has allowed for such an inherent feeling of acceptance than what I've felt here.

Ah think ae the blue water n white sands ae the Caribbean; the view fae ma bedroom windae right across Falkirk n Stirling tae the Ochil Hills beyond. A view freed fae the constraints ae the narrow streets, but ye always hink ye know where ye'd rather be.

Realisin that he'd created a moment's silence between us, Gabriel chirps in, Then again, these feelings might just be the drugs, he smiles. They're a lotta fun. Do you wanna take some?

Ah then reach intae ma bag n search fur the ket. If there's one thing that cin numb the throbbin pain that emanates fae ma shin, it's that. Ah pour some ae the salt-lookin substance ontae the back ae ma hand n snort; dae the same fur Gabriel. We watch in silence as the smudged ship continues tae hover its way across the horizon.

Gabriel leans over tae kiss me. It's long n deep; all the while ma hands run through the back ae his mullet. Our bodies ur so entwined thit ah cin feel his heightened heartbeat poondin back against ma own. The water continues tae lap gently against the shore.

We lie fur a few mair minutes until the floatiness kicks in n the pain fades away.

Right, dae you wanty go see Lorde wi me? ah say.

Yeah, he goes.

N then we ur off.

Even though ah cin see that ma feet ur movin, it feels like ah um floatin as ah make ma way tae the main stage. It's as if we ur in control ae the crowd, the seas part as we navigate the flow ae the water.

We huv pissed aboot so much thit when we arrive, Lorde is nearin the end ae her set. Gabriel and I stand arms aroond each other as the sun sets behind the stage, the sky its own light show ae golds n blues behind the intricately designed production which forms Lorde's superstar finale. During

'Perfect Places', Gabriel leans intae me n goes, I couldn't think of a more perfect place to be, with a more perfect person. Ah think this is ripped straight oot the pages ae an airport romance novel n write the cringe aff as doon tae the Mandy, but smile n say Aye! as ah lean in fur another kiss.

The sun slumps below the skyline n the lights strung between metal poles twist n curve within ma peripheral vision, leadin oot ae bounds fae the festival n intae the hills ae Barca beyond. They are where ah need tae be.

Gabriel goes tae me, I need to head to the bathrooms—join me?

Sure thing, ma man.

We wander once again to the portaloos. The world hus become a kaleidoscope ae colour in which ah currently have no agency, ah um on a floating rollercoaster that only intensifies as ah move another bump ae ket tae ma nostril. As we finally pull intae the toilets, ah head fur one ae the cubicles by masel. As ah stand tae dae ma business, when it feels like the waterworks might actually start tae flow, the sensation suddenly disappears. Frustrated, ah groan, which prompts laughter fae ootside. Ah sit n hope fur gravity tae take hold n work its magic. After aboot five minutes, there's a *drip, drip, drip*, against the plastic pan n a massive sigh ae relief fae me.

Standin at the entrance tae the toilets, ah wait fur Gabriel. Ten, fifteen minutes pass n he doesnae appear. It's wi this that ah once again notice the lights ae the festival highlight the loomin hills ae Barca in the distance. Ah cin only imagine whit a spectacle the city must look like fae the top.

Ma quest is set.

~

Venturin back intae the blocks ae Barcelona, the walls ae the buildins seem tae breathe. Wi each movement ah make toward ma towerin destination, they seem tae reach oot further intae the street. The windows contort intae crude faces as they curve oot over ma heid, as if threatenin tae consume me. Ah turn tae the concrete n lay aw ten ae ma fingertips against it, lightly draggin them doon the wall. The buildins seem to retreat intae themselves. Flesh n blood hus won against the beatin heart ae Barca's blocks. Wi this, the paths turn to gravel, n ma ascent begins.

Ah stand wi ma hands restin oan the stone edge ae El Turó de la Rovira. The dawn dilutes the hues ae light n turns Barca intae a pastel portrait; pinks, purples, peaches. Reachin intae ma bag, ah grab ma pack ae cigarettes n light one. Ah inhale deeply and blow the fumes oot intae the sky. The wisps claw toward the cosmos, longin tae make their way fur the last ae the stars visible.

The views fi up here ur absolutely stunnin; ye cin see right across the city tae the endless sea beyond. Fae amongst the vast sprawl ae blocks in front ae me jut oot two immediately recognisable buildins. Aw roads lead tae the Sagrada Familia; and the Gherkin, which isnae actually it's name, ah've just taken tae callin it that cause it's near ma hostel, looks like the one in London n ah cin remember it when ahm fucked. It's like a beacon ae light at six in the mornin when ketted oot yer nut.

You definitely ur ketted oor yer nut the noo, int ye? calls a recognisable voice fae behind me.

Bet ye didnae expect tae see me here, did ye?

Behind me is masel; masel as ah look the noo.

You're no real, ah say.

Of course ahm no real! he responds, laughin. But we're one n the same, n that's real enough.

So, yer nearly at the end ae yer time in Barca, he says.

The weight ae this knowledge bears doon oan me like the heaviest ae burdens.

Yep, back tae Falkirk, ah respond.

Dae ye ever hink aboot it?

Hink aboot whit? ah turn tae look at masel, wi an eyebrow crooked.

Whit could huv been.

Wi this statement, tunnel vision takes over ma peripheral. Barca itself, in all its pastel painted beauty, becomes an amalgamation ae greys, suppression n lost time as ah double over wi ma stomach churnin.

Just breathe, mate, he says tae masel. Take yer time.

Once ah huv regained composure, ah look masel directly in the eye and choke oot through a sob, Aw the time. Years huv gone by. Who wouldnae?

He looks at me sadly. That person is gone. Long gone. Ye do realise that even if ye went back n were able tae change hings, ye couldnae huv the life ye hink? Everyhin you went through hus shaped you. The strength you've shown would cripple most cunts. Don't grieve fur the cunt ye coulda been. Be proud ae the cunt ye ur the day.

Goosebumps coat ma skin fae heid tae tae; ah begin tae weep.

He plucks ma cigarette fae me n takes a puff. When ah turn tae look at him once more, he is gone.

The sun continues tae creep its way across the horizon. In the distance, sunbeams shimmer aff the ripples ae the sea.

Titilayo Farukuoye

UNICORN RUMINANT
After Rick Dove

The last unicorn
just more stabby with their horn
Obviously smells of grass and dirt

Brr Ptch brrPTChbrr (chewing sounds)
What would it sound like
if horses spat up grass again
ruminating?

Prick your ears! What's that?

The liminal sound of the cashier's
at… [insert your favourite shop here (obvi it's Lidl)]

UNICORN AT THE CASHIER'S

Why? Cause also unicorns gotta get their cigarettes from
somewhere…
Stomping in the queue, chewing some greenery in their left
mouth corner

didn't pay for it ofc
But who would pay for the tops of some radishes anyway?

I once had a cashier pluck them right off my veg
Or do you need them?! they'd asked, I felt embarrassed
   the hoarder in me screamed a loud *YESSSSS*
But a cool, casual me, laughed a generous *nah*, his smile, lit
   bored eyes slit,
mouth corner wide and open.

The cashier was unfaced either way
my   green   heads   disappeared   under   the   counter
   inside a bin out of sight.

~

Now I'd plucked off my green tops in advance
To avoid the waste!

Threw in some carrots and radishes
you know what late-night shopping on a hungry stomach's
like

Stopped at that middle aisle too
after two weeks, I am still looking for a suitable horseshoe
BUT NO LUCK THIS TIME

Even   unicorns   gotta   get   their   cigarettes   somewhere...

I scratch my belly, dreamy
My hinder hoof almost catches the person behind me in
   the queue
They squeak

I only notice the shrieking
too late. *Mind your space! Wasn't it COVID 19 2 minutes ago?!*
Why do all of these people need to be up in my behind
    ALL the time…?!
I'm not gonna lie
I've got a pretty full, round, juicy ass
gorgeous, blue back-braid-horsetail in my tail as well.

Would be hard to resist
I presume.

But a unicorn needs to get their cigarettes from somewhere!

How long til they'll tell me off for smoking
whilst still in the queue?

Ripped open the pack with my teeth!
or did I gently trample it to kick it open?

Definitely no teen that helped me, no kid that even
snuck me a lighter, *no! no… (none of that)*

Unicorns and cigarettes
What else would I be up to on a Thursday night?

Matthew Kinlin

RIVER

Parts of the Tollcross, an area in east Glasgow, were formerly known as *Egypt* and are still marked so on a number of maps. The name is said to have been derived from a farm that existed at one time in the area, operated by a former soldier who had been stationed in Egypt.

On Wednesday, August 19th 2020, a river in Tollcross Park began to change colour. The water turned bright purple on Friday August 21st.

The Scottish Environment Protection Agency (SEPA) stated: 'On Wednesday, August 19, SEPA received reports that water in Tollcross Burn was an inky black colour. Our officers are investigating and understand that the discolouration had ceased, until receiving reports of a purple hue in the same watercourse on Friday August, 21.'

It was reported in the *Daily Record* that 'shocked locals scrambled to the banks of the Tollcross Burn in Tollcross Park to watch on as the flowing water turned a bright violet shade on Friday.'

The following seven observations were audio recorded a month later with accompanying notes.

~

RECORDING_1.mp3

Ultraviolet is faster than visible light. It's like a kaleidoscope that spins faster and faster until the shapes disappear. I walked towards Tollcross Burn and the light refracted into a multitude of opalescent patterns across the back of someone's North Face jacket. It was a midday and suddenly the sun fractured and resembled a red scorpion. I have known scorpions for my whole life. My younger sister kept scorpions as a teenager. The tank for the scorpions was too big for her bedroom so it went in the living room. Slowly, our house in Shawlands became known as the *House of the Scorpion*. On her eleventh birthday, she shaved her head and called herself *King Scorpion (1)*. My sister named the scorpions after all the boys she liked. The first five brothers were named after NSYNC *(2)*. There was Justin, as in Justin Timberlake, and then JC, Joey, Chris and Lance. Lance was the gay one who tried to go into space. He wanted to send teenagers into space as part of a youth programme and she wrote emails to him, saying she was proud that he had come out as gay and about her favourite constellations: Cassiopeia, Ursa Minor. She was a Gemini.

1. Scorpion II, or King Scorpion, was a ruler of Upper Egypt from c. 3200–3000 BCE.
2. NSYNC, sometimes stylised as *NSYNC or 'N Sync, were a boyband created by Lou Pearlman who had formed Backstreet Boys. Pearlman was sentenced to prison in 2008 for running one of the largest Ponzi schemes in American history.

~

RECORDING_2.mp3

The glasshouse in Tollcross Park was filled with many insects that afternoon. Wasps and dragonflies levitated above roses in crystalline spires. My eyes were beginning to stream due to the pollen. I have always been sickly. I once had a CT scan *(1)* at the Royal Infirmary and it felt like climbing inside a microwave. As I walked towards Tollcross Burn, I could feel my nose begin to bleed because of the allergies. The river was entirely covered in bumblebees *(2)*. I always get nosebleeds on aeroplanes. My friend Rashida says the nosebleeds are a bad omen. She showed me a film called *Final Destination (3)* where a boy has a premonition that they are all going to die on an aeroplane. Him and his friends are kicked off the flight because he is shouting that they are all about to die. Afterwards, the plane explodes. He was right but it's not enough to save them because it was their destiny to die that day and no one escapes their destiny. Maybe the nosebleed is telling me to get off the plane but I just sit there. I do as I'm told. It's the blood that tries to leave.

1. A computerized tomography (CT) scan uses x-ray images to create crosssectional images of the human body.
2. Unlike humans, bumblebees are able to see ultraviolet light. Many flowers emit a UV light that guides the bee to its pollen and nectar.
3. The original idea for *Final Destination* was written by Jeffrey Reddick as a spec script for *The X-Files*. Some DVDs of the film contained a game called *Death Clock*.

~

RECORDING_3.mp3

It didn't affect me as much as the others. I just found the water really jarring. I had come up from Househillwood on the bus, past Silverburn shopping centre. There are many strange happenings in Househillwood. Someone once did a Ouija board in their kitchen to contact the Earl of Clanbrassil who had owned Househill Park. Instead, they spoke with the cousin of a Pictish princess *(1)* that was deaf and died in the 6th century. There was a man in Househillwood called Percy, short for Percival, who sang a rhyme about the weather: *Mackerel sky, mackerel sky. Never long wet and never long dry.* I described Tollcross Burn to him and he gave me a book from one his shelves called *Beyond the Mauve Zone (2)*. He died a week later on the hottest day of the year. We all stood indoors. The paramedics wore sunglasses and unbuttoned their sleeves.

1. The Picts were an ancient people known to have lived in northern and north-eastern Scotland. Their kingdom was known as Pictland.
2. *Beyond the Mauve Zone* is a work from Kenneth Grant, Thelemic magician and founder of the Typhonian Order, published in 1995.

RECORDING_4.mp3

A vampire is the most romantic invention of the human imagination. We had just finished watching an anime series called *Revolutionary Girl Utena (1)* and come to see the famous rose garden in Tollcross Park. We spent the summer reading the poetry of Charles Baudelaire. Summer was our most haunted season. In our Gorbals flat, we dressed as pale French boys and read aloud about corpses rotting inside tombs of lavender. I heard the words as we approached the bank of Tollcross Burn. *Rappelez-vous l'objet que nous vîmes, mon âme, ce beau matin d'été si doux (2).* The roses were spinning in ultraviolet cyclones. Afterwards at home, we undressed quietly. Vampires are unable to see their own reflections. They can only imagine and feel the shape of their faces with their fingertips. It's like trying to make your way through a room in total darkness. We climbed into the bathtub and described the colour of each other's eyes. Hers were grey. Mine were auburn.

1. *Revolutionary Girl Utena* is a Japanese animated series about Utena Tenjou, a teenage girl who wears male clothing. In each episode, Utena is drawn into a sword duel to win the hand of Anthy Himemiya, a mysterious girl known as the Rose Bride.
2. C. Baudelaire, *The Carcass.* Trans. *My love, do you recall the object which we saw, that fair, sweet, summer morn!*

RECORDING_5.mp3

I had spent the afternoon in Tollcross Park drinking cans of Dragon Soop *(1)*: Red Kola, Blue Raspberry and Venom. The river looked like my favourite one, which was *Wicked Watermelon*. I bent down behind a bush and my piss came out bright silver. The river made me feel an incredible sense of fear. I thought about a scene from *Scream 2 (2)* where the reporter Gale Weathers is running down a corridor. The killer is coming after her. I was too drunk and had to get back home.

I left the other observers at the side of Tollcross Burn and got onto a bus heading back to Govan. Sat on the bus, I took out a deodorant can of Dolce & Gabbana's *Light Blue* and sprayed the entire bottle. I listened to the little screams coming out. I started from the tip of my trainers and sprayed all the way to the end of my ponytail. The smell was making the other passengers angry as I dissolved inside Mediterranean waves of juniper and bergamot. My body was on fire. I thought to myself: *I am not here. I am not in Govan (3).*

1. Dragon Soop is an alcoholic drink fermented with vodka, caffeine, taurine and guarana.
2. *Scream 2* is the 1997 follow-up to Wes Craven's original meta-slasher. At one point, the character of Randy Meeks explains, 'The entire horror genre was destroyed by sequels.'
3. The earliest record of Govan comes from a 12th century Latin source that records a place near Dumbarton Rock named *Ouania*. It is believed to have been reconstructed in Cumbric language as *(G)uovan*.

RECORDING_6.mp3

The river looked like the pages of my diary. When I am having a bad day, I write in purple ink. I call these days *purple* or *a purple day*. The purple stands for danger. It always has. As a child, my mother would put on *Barney & Friends* and I would run and hide. An imaginary dinosaur was singing on the television. It looked like a crocodile. What scared me was that the children had brought Barney to life through their imaginations. They possessed a terrible power. This purple crocodile was the same colour as a frightening book my grandmother owned called *The Lady with the Magic Eyes* *(1)*. As an adult, I read more about crocodiles. In a museum in Dundee, I saw an ancient parchment of a god with a crocodile's head *(2)*. It made me think of Barney & Friends and being a child in bed at night. I would lie there and try not think about Barney or about anything purple, all night long. It's difficult not to think about purple. You have to be careful what you dream about.

1. John Symonds' biography explores the life of Madame Blavatsky, the 19th century Russian aristocrat and founder of the Theosophical Society, known for dressing in the magical colour of purple.
2. The Egyptian god Sobek has a human body with the head of a crocodile. As part of the cult of Sobek, some crocodiles were executed at the temple of *Crocodilopolis* and mummified in a grand ritual.

RECORDING_7.mp3

When Tollcross Burn changed colour, we sat in silent mediation afterwards. One of us spoke about the intersex god Hapi *(1)* who announced the annual flooding of the Nile. We looked south towards Cambuslang where the Giza Necropolis was shining inside lavender twilight. Walking towards the river bank, we were surrounded by beautiful Khmer statues, a child cradling a serpent. In an empty carpark, we found a sarcophagus choked in ylang-ylang flowers. Beneath its feet lay an offering to the gods: a binbag filled with damp and unused fireworks. We set the entire bag alight and watched it

fizz and smoke. It tore itself apart in pink and green flames.
We dragged the sarcophagus onto a boat on the River Clyde
and smashed it into pieces. The sun was rising. We smiled
and pulled scabs from our knees. Our legs were covered in
purple emperor butterflies. At a flat in Denniston, we ate
edibles and watched *Lucifer Rising (2)*. Orange UFOs floated
above the Great Sphinx. Tollcross Burn was like the scene in
Apocalypse Now where the boys are firing bullets into purple
smoke *(3)*. We looked towards the Atlantic and repeated the
mantra of Captain Benjamin L. Willard. We spat the words
into each other's mouth. *Everyone gets everything he wants (4)*.

1. Hapi is an androgynous god with a large belly and
   drooping breasts. They wear a fake ceremonial beard.
2. *Lucifer Rising* is a short film of Kenneth Anger released
   in 1980 that presents an invocation of Lucifer as
   understood by Aleister Crowley as the light-bearing
   god or morning star.
3. Colonel Kurtz's final words derive from the Joseph
   Conrad's source novel, *Heart of Darkness*, which asks:
   *Did he live his life again in every detail of desire, temptation,
   and surrender during that supreme moment of complete
   knowledge?*
4. One of the books seen open on Kurtz's desk is James
   Frazer's *The Golden Bough*. Francis Ford Coppola has
   linked the ending of *Apocalypse Now* with Frazer's
   concept of the Fisher King, a figure in Arthurian legend
   tasked with the guarding of the Holy Grail. He must
   swim up the river and kill the king to become the king.

Adi Novak

SALT LINES

John Brown never gives another name. Not when he's soaked in sea spray and fevered sweat, exposed at the surgeon's order. Not when his mate, upon discovery of more sally-ports than expected, stumbles to report Brown's condition to their Commander. Pulling on a dress, handed to him by the Commander in lieu of the form of punishment he'd expected, he sticks to his guns. His name is John Brown. This is the name that will be written in Commander Thomas Phillips' log on Saturday 18th November, 1693. It won't matter how much his identity is debated by academics of the future, or how much they inevitably misunderstand his reasons for doing what he does. They will always be forced to get at least one thing about him right.

Brown's mate comes to see him later that night. It's not easily done. Brown has been placed in a small cabin for the sake of decency, though if anyone had truly wanted to keep his secret, they would have allowed him to return to the rest of the men. But now that he is discovered, things must be done properly. He must force his handsome body into the dresses, itching and nauseous. When the tentative knock comes, his hands are stinging from a day of scrubbing the Commander's linens. His skin is used to the brine and twisted ropes, but this is something new.

It takes several minutes of hushed pleading through the keyhole before Brown lets his mate in. Even then, he's not sure. This is the man who turned him in, after all, despite three months of friendship. And should something happen now, Brown's not sure that anyone would give much of a damn. But there's a part of him, perhaps, that wants to make sure he's understood by at least one person before they reach Cape Coast.

'I'm sorry,' his mate tells him. Brown stands quietly, hands instinctively moving towards pockets that aren't there. He folds them behind his back, instead. 'I had to, you wouldn't have been safe if anyone else had found out.'

'I got this far,' says Brown.

His mate nods. 'You had me fooled. You're certainly bold, for fourteen. I'll give you that.' His eyes roam over Brown. Searching. 'You still stand like a lad. You don't have to, you know.'

Brown shifts. 'It's just how I stand,' he says. 'And I'm not a lad.'

His mate's mouth lifts at the side, the beginning of a laugh. 'I know that now, I—'

'I'll be three and twenty this spring.'

'Three and twenty?' Here, his mate does laugh. Turns away in disbelief, hands on his hips. 'Over the left! You know you've got a year on me?'

The gale died away about an hour before this conversation, leaving nothing for the sails besides the few occasional gusts of breeze. So the cabin doesn't creak, and the ship doesn't pitch as it had in the height of Brown's fever. The candle flame burns tall and steady. In the relative stillness, for just a moment, Brown can almost believe that time has stopped.

That the fates have allowed him this pause in which he can make a move; that constructing some plan to escape is still possible.

Sweat builds under his arms and on his lower back, soaking into fabric. Brown breathes slowly, deeply, and wills the lightness in his head to pass. His mate faces him again. 'You're well now, I take it?'

Brown nods once.

'Good, that's good. I was worried it might be something more serious, you understand. I hope you'll forgive me for involving Mr Gordon and the Commander. I never intended to cause you any trouble.'

'Right.'

The two of them hold one another's gaze for a while. Brown sways in place, almost imperceptibly. Even through the haze of lingering illness he's aware of his shadow on the wall, juddering in all the wrong shapes.

His mate is still getting his head around the age revelation. He's also most likely prodding at the edge of what he'll never truly comprehend, but trying for some kind of understanding anyway.

'I suppose it all worked out for the best in the end, anyhow.'

'What do you mean?'

'Well,' his mate hesitates, then nods in the general area of Brown's torso. 'No need to pretend, now, is there?' He doesn't get a response, so he continues. 'No more sleeping with the rest of us huffers. I'd do anything to get my own private quarters.'

Brown would really love to explain what is is his mate has got so wrong, but his vision is beginning to swim. Perhaps finding meaningful connection was overly optimistic, after all. All things considered, he shouldn't be surprised. But in the moments before he passes out, he's still disappointed.

Aristotle's Masterpiece: Or, The Secrets of Generation was published nine years previously, and, due to raging popularity, is due for a reprint. It's entirely possible that a volume happens to be on board at the same time as Brown; let's say Commander Phillips pays a visit to the Hand and Sceptre in the month leading up to the *Hannibal's* departure from London, and, on a whim, decides to purchase a copy. It's safe to assume he doesn't realise how little time he'll actually have for reading. Of those who had a choice in the matter, no one would get on the boat if they knew just how badly wrong the voyage would go—but he doesn't have the power of foresight. He believes he's competent. It costs him ten shillings.

By the time Brown has been discovered they've nearly reached Pico Teneriffe.

The hours of daylight are long. The opportunity for reading is greater than expected.

Perhaps the book has been left behind in Brown's temporary holding cell, forgotten in the chaos. The room was never intended to be used like this, after all. The irony of extra space being available on a ship where seven hundred men, women and children are chained in tightly-packed shelves is sickening. It doesn't make sense. But there it is, the second book down in a small pile by the back corner.

Alternatively, Brown's mate catches onto a truer aspect of his friend's laddish state, and seeing the volume somewhere on the ship, manages to slip it into his jacket. Whether he knows why is beside the point; he can see that Brown isn't relishing in his new-found role as laundry maid and feels rather rotten about the whole situation. He leaves it just outside Brown's door. Does the old knock and run.

Or perhaps it's done with crueller intent. By whom is uncertain, though it won't be Phillips himself. Once a place for the anomaly is found and is seen to be in the correct clothes, he rids his mind of the entire matter. The state of the weather is far more concerning at this point, and an outbreak of the bloody flux is tearing through the slaves chained below. He's also the kind of man to grossly underestimate Brown's ability to read. In any case, he's distracted enough to not notice a single book missing from his collection, newly-purchased or not.

To its credit, the book does propose some interesting theories. The idea that men can, on occasion, be at fault just as much as women when failing to conceive a child seems rather modern and is appreciated by Brown. The wood engravings, on the other hand, particularly in the final few pages, bring the tone down somewhat. This isn't to say they're not entertaining—but the inclusion of a 16th century report of a winged-mutant-baby (complete with horns and bird feet) does lessen the rest of the book's validity.

Brown wishes this element of absurdity would ease the churning in his stomach when he finds the chapter that explains, in great detail, every fault he possesses and the reasons for their occurrence. According to the learned and ingenious physicians, a lot of the responsibility lies with his parents. His mother didn't spend enough time lying on her right side in the days after his conception. She didn't keep warm enough. Or perhaps she was too warm. His father should have eaten more parsnips and artichokes, and they both had overactive imaginations.

The moon must have also been in Libra or Aquarius.

Hermaphrodite. The word is italicised on the page. An emphasis. Clear, curled contempt even without verbal delivery. The result of his parents' failings. Now his own.

Brown continues to read the book, cover to cover. It does nothing for his mental state but it's either this or re-washing his captor's shirts. The author (somehow Brown suspects it's not actually Aristotle) repeats themself a fair amount. It also becomes apparent that *hermaphrodite* is a convenient label to affix to anything that strays outside a very specific ideal for a human. Namely, anything other than deathly pale, mostly hairless, of a particular persuasion regarding partners, and in possession of four functioning limbs. Brown excels in at least three of these criteria for monstrosity.

Mermaids are included under this umbrella term. Or, at least, creatures which appear to be close to what Brown has heard described by fellow crew members. He studies the thick, black lines. Repeated, curved, carved into wood and filled with ink—hours of work have been put into depicting these grotesque beings. Brown looks at the scaly tail of one unlikely individual and pictures his own body changing. In his imagination, he wills himself to morph below the waist, legs joining to become one thick, strong appendage. No room for confusion; everyone knows a tail when they see one. When he throws himself off the side of the ship he won't drown, or be eaten by sharks, as he knows has already been the fate for many on this voyage. The water will welcome him. It is unknowable from the surface. Vast and endlessly varied.

~

By Wednesday 22nd November, Brown is finished with *Aristotle's Masterpiece: Or, The Secrets of Generation*. He's now in the process of burning it, page by page. He has started with the illustrations and is working his way backwards, though since the ship is wooden he's taking it slowly. Just in case.

At four a.m., someone in the crow's nest sights a ship between the *Hannibal* and the shoreline. Brown doesn't know this yet, because his quarters are on the wrong side. All he can see, should he look out of his very small window, is open water.

The ship is huge, and despite its English ensign the crew of the *Hannibal* are nervous. It's the tail-end of the 17th century, though. Even the largest ships move fairly slowly, and so their anxiety is drawn out over several long hours. This gives them time to tidy all the hammocks out of the way, get the hatch ports off, the guns ready, and bring the *Hannibal* around to the north. The sun beats down on their necks; the ocean goes on in its glinting, blinding and beautiful. By approximately midday, the ship is finally visible to Brown and confirmed to be an enemy vessel.

In his journal, Commander Phillips details the attack in a tone that suggests the pirates are no match for the *Hannibal*. He's sloshed at the time. While it's true that in the end, the pirates sail away and the *Hannibal* doesn't sink, it can't really be considered a victory.

The fight lasts six hours. Limbs are blown off, men are shredded by violently splintered sections of the ship, and the sails, masts, and rigging are all but destroyed. Mr Gordon is the only surgeon.

John Brown doesn't appear in any future written records. For all intents and purposes, he is gone. It is possible that he doesn't survive this attack, or that his illness returns to finish him off. The hygiene standards on the *Hannibal* are famously dismal. But an alternative fate is also entirely plausible. He has already spent a significant portion of his life slipping under the radar of document-writers, after all. Gazes will continue to pass over him throughout history.

When he walks out of the cabin it's to a scene of utter chaos. No one notices.

There are at least five bodies within his line of sight. He makes his way to the smallest and cleanest. The most whole. He removes the jacket and breeches, and quietly rejoins the crew. With the current noise-level, this isn't difficult.

Brown has no particular loyalty to the *Hannibal* crew (perhaps with the exception of his mate, but at this time it's unclear whether he's alive). He certainly couldn't care less about the success of Phillips. But he knows there are still hundreds of lives worth protecting below deck, and the water levels are constantly rising. He makes his way down towards the chain pump as quickly as possible, dodging panicked men and debris, and throws himself into keeping it going.

Within minutes his body is in pain. Muscles strain to move a weight beyond anything he's dealt with before. He's shorter than the other men. Further to stretch. Water higher around his legs. If he passes out now, he'll drown.

In this exact moment, all Brown can focus on is the agony ripping through his shoulders. The thickness of sweat, blood, and salt in the air. He can't know that change is coming—for those in his immediate vicinity, or, with time, on a wider scale. But he senses something. A shared rage, perhaps, stirring in those around him. Disgust at the rising deaths on this disastrous voyage—soon to amount to four hundred, caused by Phillips and his kind. An anger that will simmer and build, finally breaking into action in 1697, on New Year's Day, when the *Hannibal*'s second and final attempted slave-trade will be ended by a mutinous crew.

And though he's unable to put a name to it at this time, something has shifted within him, too, strengthening with each volley. It thunders through his chest. His ears ring with it. Somewhere nearby, possibilities freed from now-burnt pages blow into the open ocean. Ashes move with ease, the finest layer coating waves. They carry on each eddy towards the pirates. Some pass on. And some slap up against the the underbelly of the ship, find a crevice, and take hold.

Paul Brownsey

SHOWER SCENE

The moment I first saw him all those years ago, it was different from all the other times I'd spotted someone in the bar that I might want to sleep with. Usually I had to do a mental makeover on a guy in order to persuade myself that he matched my template for the person I would love for ever. But with Jeff, that was unnecessary. The short neatly-parted hair, the black-framed glasses, the slight defensive smile as he sipped whisky, the neat moustache that harked back to an older tradition of men's facial hair (say, Clark Gable)—for once, the hope in my head was there in the flesh. I pushed towards him through the crowd in the Duke of Wellington. Already he was so familiar to me, so deeply embedded in my life, that I knew exactly how the musculature of his chest occupied the golden mean, neither skinny-weedy nor beefed-up like obscene armour.

Before I could reach him, a practised old queen called Maxie ('Maxine') Dinnett shimmied past him, brazenly miming a crotch-to-crotch rub. '*Not* tonight, I'm afraid. My labours are demanded, alas, on the night shift at a most superior eventide home. But I'll always be willing to assist *you* in the shower. I'm sure a shower scene would be right up your alley.' Maxie widened his eyes in a flirtatious question, pursed his lips in a little kissing motion.

As I raged that this decent ordinary guy should be the victim of Maxie's degrading campery, I realised why he'd seemed so familiar.

I'd seen the guy naked in a porn magazine.

Oh, compared to what is available today *porn* feels too strong a word for *HIM Exclusive* in the 1970s. Full-frontal nudity, yes, but no sex. Yet the images could still harness you. There was a shot of a man leaning against a bookcase that had the power religious images can have over the devout. He was holding a book (you couldn't see the title) but his attention was drawn by someone off-camera to his left, to whom he was giving a smile which radiated all the open-hearted decency and trust, all the delight in another person, that you could ever hope for. In that smile, in his black-framed glasses, in his neatly-parted hair, was total ignorance that he was being photographed naked. He wasn't the sort to expose his cock for perving over in a soft-porn magazine. You were viewing him in his ordinary life.

But I couldn't just go up to him and say I'd seen his picture in *HIM Exclusive*. I'd sound like a creep, whereas I knew that what I was going to initiate was a for-ever-and-ever relationship. As I dithered, the guy caught my eye, nodded towards the exiting Maxie, and said, 'If I thought that was my future, I'd be out of here like a shot.'

'But it doesn't have to be your future,' I said, and we shook hands.

After we'd made love again the next morning, he said, 'I wonder if we'd have connected if that old queen hadn't given us common ground.' It was a moment of confidence in each other, instead of the polite awkwardness of a one-night stand winding down. This was the moment to tell him I'd recognised him from *HIM Exclusive*.

But what he'd said after Maxie's departure checked me: *If I thought that was my future, I'd be out of here like a shot.* Which meant he was so innocent about the gay world that he'd seriously believed everyone might be like Maxie. Someone so innocent couldn't have got to be a model for a gay soft-porn magazine. So I kept quiet about the photo and we made our plans to meet again.

As soon as I'd waved him down the close stairs, though, I needed to find that photo, needed to check whether after all it could have been Jeff in *HIM Exclusive.* In those days, my parents visited every autumn, and before they arrived I would clear everything incriminating out of my flat. Copies of *Gay News* and other gay magazines, the novels by Rechy and Genet and Isherwood—these I used to put in an old grey cardboard suitcase, lugged safely up into the communal loft-space reached through a trapdoor above the top-storey landing. I needed to get up there.

And I realised I had the wrong take on *If I thought that was my future, I'd be out of here like a shot.* He hadn't turned and left. So he must have known already that not everyone in the gay world was a fluttery self-hating queen like Max; must have known that there were people around like himself, like me, guys who just wanted to fall in love with another guy. And he'd known the phrase *old queen.* So he was experienced after all. Drawn into porn, posing naked in someone's flat while the photographer clicked away, sex with the photographer while other models watched, then these other guys moving in on Jeff, an orgy photographed for raunchier magazines than *HIM Exclusive*—

But this was jealousy, a bad emotion. No, I shouldn't go hunting for the incriminating photo. That was an easy decision to make, because of all our love and excitement. And he was charming to my parents.

Of course, we talked about our pasts, as lovers do. But if he didn't want to bring up his past in porn, that was his right. As someone who loved him, the thing for me to do was to pretend I didn't know.

It was in the euphoria of buying a place together two years later that the silly, niggling question came surging up again. A couple of days before I moved house, Jeff was helping me get down stuff that I'd stored in the communal loft-space. We'd borrowed step-ladders from Angela in the flat opposite and I went up through the trapdoor. It was so exciting, we two guys in love working together on our move into a united future, that as I handed down to him the grey cardboard suitcase, which had been permanently in the loft since I'd met him, I said, 'There's a magazine in there I want to show you.'

He didn't say anything.

We moved into my flat the stuff we'd fetched down and I returned the stepladders to Angela. Back in my flat I clicked open the suitcase. There they were, the stack of copies of *HIM Exclusive*, residue of a former me. 'In one of these there's a picture of my ideal man. Before I met him. Before I met you.' I was speaking very slowly as I searched, intending to flourish the crucial issue with the crucial picture at him with a ceremonial *Ta da!*

His face gave nothing away.

'It's not here.' I searched through the pile two, three times.

'Maybe you'll find it later.' He was in a hurry to get back to his flat because tea-chests were being delivered for his move. He took up some of bags of rubbish I'd sorted earlier. 'I'll put these in the bins for you on the way out.'

After he'd gone I looked in vain at every page of every copy of *HIM Exclusive* I possessed. Could it be that there never had been such a picture? Lovers like to think of their love as predestined, foreshadowed, its foundations laid down, both in themselves and outside them, long before they ever met. Had my mind somehow projected back into the magazine, into pre-Jeff days, the sense of him that was with me all the time now, the sense of his body as mine, the image of it?

Then it struck me: as I handed the suitcase down to him from the loft and said what I'd said, he must have guessed what was coming. So while I was returning the stepladders to Angela—and, yes, Angela and I had talked for a while about the people who'd bought my flat, so he had time—he'd opened the suitcase, removed the crucial issue, put it in one of the bags of rubbish he'd taken down to the bins in the back court. I started down the common stair to retrieve it.

I halted on the stairs. If Jeff suspected I knew about his nude posing but had still gone to the trouble of smuggling the crucial evidence out from under my nose, it must have really troubled him. He knew it was a blot on the integrity so plain in the photo. He stole it to prevent positive identification, maybe scared I'd have second thoughts about settling down with him if I knew definitively about his tarnished past. I could assure him that positive identification wouldn't make any difference, but with us on the brink of our new life together in our new home, wasn't it time to let the whole business go? It belonged to the prehistory of our love and didn't matter now, one way or the other. I went back up to what would soon be my flat no longer, content that the binmen should take the magazine to be incinerated out of our lives. I'd done something to make sure our relationship would last forever.

And for many years, that was that. When the man who embodies your dream is there every day, waking up next to you, what does it matter when and how that dream first entered your brain?

One day, ten or eleven years later, out of the blue, I was suddenly convinced he'd stuffed the magazine inside his shirt instead of putting it in a bag of rubbish.

Once, in the dentist's chair, I wondered whether I'd omitted to put it in the loft-bound suitcase and my visiting parents, to whom I had not yet come out, had found it in a pile of newspapers and taken it away. Yet I couldn't remember any new overlay of concern in their dealings with me.

A couple of years after that, as I sat outside the room where I was about to be interviewed for a new job, I remembered that, when I lived in my old flat, Angela's husband left her for another woman. Maybe, packing up to leave, retrieving stuff from the communal loft-space with only a hand-held torch for light, he mistook my suitcase for something of his, opened it, realised his mistake, but before he clicked it shut, the copy of *HIM Exclusive* with Jeff's nude photo slid out unnoticed and fell down between joists. Where, perhaps, it still lay amid sooty dust and cobwebs, in darkness.

It wasn't until the day we got married that the question really flared up again. At the Registration Office, a general purposes room had been set aside for Jeff and me before the ceremony in the main hall. There was a formal table and chairs, a coffee table, some armchairs, a bookcase containing old telephone books, old legal volumes, local directories, even a Bible. I went for a pee. When I returned, Jeff was leaning against the bookcase, glancing at some book he'd taken down to fill in the time. I couldn't see what it was. He turned to his left, like the guy in the photo, and gave me exactly the smile that I remembered, the smile of total trust in me and delight in me, and he stood in exactly the same pose. Of course, he was several decades older, in a dove-grey suit. But what I saw was the naked body from *HIM Exclusive*.

'The same pose!' I cried, utterly startled.

'What do you mean?'

I could have invented something about an actor in a film still, passed it off as just a coincidence, but I couldn't lie to him when I was about to marry him. So, at last, I told him about the nude photo; about how I'd recognised him from it in The Duke of Wellington. 'You never told me about that,' I said, more accusingly than I'd intended.

'Perhaps,' he said, 'because whatever photo you saw, it wasn't of me. For God's sake! Has that been bugging you? Come here.' He put the book down—the Bible, I noticed—pulled me to him and kissed me very gently. Just at that moment the Registrar entered, stood smiling us into attention, and we got in place to follow her into the main hall for the ceremony in front of our guests.

But I was thinking: though I couldn't lie to him about the photo just as we were getting married, could he lie to me? It felt obscene even to suspect such a thing as we exchanged vows, but, once again, I really, really had to see that photo and check.

But how?

Since *HIM Exclusive* had been defunct for decades, writing to the publishers for a back issue wasn't on. ('The one containing a solo nude photo of a guy by a bookcase, glasses, moustache, looking away to the left, medium cock, not circumcised'?) And having trekked out to where I used to live, picturing the crucial magazine still lying between the joists, I discovered that the whole block had been demolished, a shopping mall in its place.

When Jeff had his stroke, I sometimes wondered, getting clothes from his wardrobe for him, whether I might come across a copy. Underwear particularly made me think of this, probably because of its absence in the photo. Perhaps I'd find the copy that was missing on that distant day when we'd got my stuff down from the loft-space, or perhaps his own copy, for if you'd posed nude for a magazine, wouldn't you keep a copy? Unless you were ashamed. Whatever; I found nothing.

The brain has a strange propensity to move along the shortest possible line from seemingly irrelevant things to its own overriding preoccupations. It was because of a TV news item about Tony Blair criticising Boris Johnson that I recovered a copy of the crucial issue. The mention of Blair sent my mind zooming first to his wife, Cherie, then onward to the memory of an old newspaper story about her selling things on eBay.

Not that I thought Cherie Blair would have been selling copies of *HIM Exclusive* on eBay. But, yes, eBay offered old copies, and there it was, the familiar cover of what I was sure was the long-lost crucial issue. When it arrived in the post, two pages seemed partly stuck together—by what, I shrank from thinking. This was the final obstacle.

But though I went at the task gently, having dampened the pages in the hope that they would peel apart easily, a large part of the surface on one side tore away, stuck to the opposite surface, leaving me with the sight of a naked body up to the waist but with nothing above the waist except raw white paper. There were no shelves behind lower part of the body, but maybe what I'd remembered as shelves was just a small wall shelf behind the shoulders.

I could hardly go to Jeff, still speech-impaired, still with limited movement from his stroke, and say, 'Hey, I just took a notion to send for this old copy of *HIM Exclusive*. It *is* you, isn't it?' If it was him, the contrast to Jeff in his damaged state was too cruel; and it would be an additional cruelty in that I'd be accusing him of having lied to me.

I heard him stirring in the bedroom, trying to get out of bed for his shower, where he could stand so long as he used his good hand to grip the shower screen but couldn't wash himself because the other hand was too weak. I hurried through to assist his hobble to the shower. Soaping him all over, hands and flannel diligent as necessary, became my means of judging whether the naked body half visible in the photo was Jeff's. He'd gained weight over the years, was flabbier and bulgier than the guy in the photo, and the hang of his lower belly above his crotch was no match for the exquisite line downwards from his navel in *HIM Exclusive*. There was more body hair now, but then, men tend to get hairier as they get older. The cock in the photo was bigger, but doesn't it shrink a bit as you get older?

Even if the face had been visible in the magazine, would there have been any chance of confirming that that face, with its blessed normality, with all its innocence, integrity, and delight in the person it saw, was that of today's Jeff, moustacheless, enduring, a bit dazed? But my hands, busy only on the routine movements of washing, knew that my poor Jeff, my lovely Jeff, was indeed the man whose image I had carried in my brain forever and even before forever began.

Pernina Jacobs

A LETTER TO NEVER BE SENT TO MY GRANDMA PLEASE GOD

I can't quite square any of this / I'm trying to fit all the pieces of my life together / like that time when I was seven / and got sick / and couldn't do the jigsaw puzzle with the man selling cabbages / because my brain fog was so bad / and I cried and mum told me it was okay / that it's hard to do easy things when you're sick / I feel like that means I've been sick for a while now / it's getting easier to do the hard things / like I can kiss a girl in public now / and yes it's cringe because pda / I just realised you don't know what pda is / it's public displays of affection / and it kind of grosses me out / but I don't know if a lot of that is internalised homophobia / and I just realised you don't know what internalised homophobia is / it's when you have taken in so much of the homophobia of the world around you / it plants itself like a seed in the pit of your body somewhere / and every time you think you've got rid of it / there comes that voice / or that feeling / telling you that something you're doing is wrong / anyway I can kiss girls in public / and in private / and in the semi-private of a dark alleyway / and the semi-public of the seats of the last train home / but it's harder to do the easy things / like change my sheets / or find a job I like / or spend ten minutes without checking my phone.

I can't quite square the me who struggled to do the puzzle / with the me I am now / like how I can't square the you / who made us nosh bags after school / and held up the loose papery skin under your arms for us to feel / they were like velvet / to the you who is filled with such vitriol / I can see it making your world smaller every year that goes by / and you sit on your sofa / in your perfectly arranged living room / and stew / you stew like the cholent you taught me to make / but the gravy's turned to tar / the pot's been on so long / just bubbling away / and I want to come and flood you with good things / like simchas and babies / but you just turn your head away from it all / and keep reducing / we'll have to throw the pot away afterwards / the char on the bottom too much even for brillo pads to scratch off / I think about the afterwards and worry / about who will find you / and who will speak / and will I get there in time / and who will do the work of the sorting / and the throwing away / and I don't know if I have the strength to box up another life / arguments over rings and candle sticks / and who takes the books back to the library / is it selfish that that's why I want you to stick around / waiting for whatever the jewish version of a hail mary is / that might change you finally?

Hannah Nicholson

WHEER

Author's note: 'Wheer' is pronounced with emphasis on the 'h' sound, to roughly imitate the 'qu' in 'queer'. It is also not unusual to see it spelled 'Hweer' which is somewhat more phonetic.

As Lerook cam intae view, we feenished aff fir brakfist an headit ootside. Hit wis a fine simmer moarnin fir a cheenge—although dey wir a breeze, da sun wis oot, dey wir barely ony cloods idda sky abön wis, an we could hear da maas skrekkin awa as dey wir fleein aroond an aboot. Da ferry chugged on at a leisurely pace, da engine girnin awa nicely.

We stood oot idda forwird deck while Marnie smokkit her fag. We looked oot taewards da starboard side, tae whaar Bressa wis slinkin slowly intae view, da lighthoose winkin awa idda distance. At da idder side da Lerook cemetery made hits appearance, followed be da rest o da toon, although we widna be able tae see muckle o da route at we'd be takkin trowe it whan we guid on da local Pride mairch da followin moarnin. Last night wis been Marnie's first shot o da nort boat, an although we wir taen wir traivel seekness peels afore we set aff hit still wisna a great experience fir her.

'I don't know how you do that every time you come home,' shö drawled atween puffs. Da springy riddish-broon curls o her hair bounced alang idda breeze.

I juist shrugged. 'I suppose I'm laekly wint wi it,' I telt her. 'Hit's aedir dis or da plane.'

'Still can't believe how expensive those flights were,' Marnie said wi disgust. 'And that was WITH your islander discount too. I guess that's what happens when you have fuck all competition, eh?'

'Yea, laeklee,' I noddit. Shö lookit at me, smeegin.

'Do you realise, Lexie,' shö telt me, 'that your accent's been getting broader the further north we've gone?'

'Hit kinda does yun,' I said. 'Hit laekly maks sense—wir comin hame eftir aa.'

'*You're* coming home, you mean,' shö gaffed. 'I'm not from here, remember? You already sound way different to usual.'

O coorse, mine an her definitions o 'usual' wir brawly different whan it cam tae da wye at I spaek. Shö wis mair wint wi me k-nappin—yun is tae say, spaekin Engleesh raedir as Shaetlan, or 'Shetlandic' as sooth fokk caa it. I haed tae do yun whan I wis awa at uni, or fokk widna understaand me as weel. I wis don me best tae introduce Marnie tae it as best I could, an shö seemed blyde, but I kent it wis still a source o great amusement tae her whan we wir in wir peerie flat tagidder an shö owerheard me on da phone tae me fokk. Engleesh isna me midder tongue, though, even if I kin still spaek it weel anoff, an I laek tae slip back intae Shaetlan laek hit's a comfy pair o auld smucks. I mind readin 'Sunset Song' fir Higher English back in secondary skule, an really relatin tae Chris Guthrie an how shö felt at dey wir twa o her, da English een at loved books an learnin, an da Scottish een at loved da fairm an da laand, an how dey wid fecht ower her haert. I fun I could relate tae yun as weel—fae I guid awa tae uni hit felt laek dey wir Shetland Lexie an Sooth Lexie, an I haed tae swap atween dem dependin on whar I wis an wha I wis wi at ony gien time. I still wisna sure whit een might end up winnin oot, an at yun time I couldna be sure how safe Shetland Lexie wis tae be oot an wheer at hame.

I fan mesel tinkin aboot me faedir. I didna keen if hit wis waar fir him at I wis taen up wi anidder lass raedir as a boy, or dat I wis taen up wi a sooth moother. But whan I first met her, hit felt richt. We wir on da sam coorse, an we bade a couple o floors apairt fae een anidder in wir halls o residence, so we saa een anidder a braw lot. I juist mind feelin dat comfortable wi her whanivver we got tae hing oot, an I fan her aesy tae spaek tae, an at I could while awa ooers doin exactly yun. I wisna even lookin fir new love—I wis haed a boyfreend back at da skule wha I wis spleet wi da simmer afore I guid tae uni first, an I suppose at I wis been hurtin a bit fae yun, but whan I wis wi Marnie yun hurt wid seem, fir juist a peerie meenit, tae heal. I telt her things I wis nivver telt ony een idder in me life, even some o me pals fae me skule days. Hit wis laekly inevitable, den, at me an her endit up gettin tagidder as 'an item', as me granny pat it whan I finally haed da guts tae tell her a peerie while laetir.

Mam, thankfully, wis fine aboot it. I wis nivver in ony doot at shö wid be—me an her wis ay haed a great relationship. Me faedir wis a different story, though. He seemed a bit pit oot, although he didna say onythin aboot it directly. Dey wir wan meetin some months afore whan dey cam awa tae veesit, an I decidit hit wis time tae introduce dem tae Marnie, fir dey wir been axin, an shö wis been axin as weel. We guid oot fir tae, an I wissed at we haedna, fir it wis akkward. Mam wis splendit as always, spaekin awa an bein really welcomin, but Dad said little, an whan he did spaek hit wis ay aedir tae me or Mam—he wid barely even look at Marnie. He didna even try tae hoid how muckle he disapproved o wis, an da hale night wis juist uncomfortable fir aabody yundir. Eftir yun incident, he'd no come back awa wi Mam ageen ivver fae den, an whan I wis been hame in yun time I wis on me ain. I wis keen tae bring Marnie hame fir da local Pride mairch, though, fir I wis nivver been tae da een idda isles, an I wantit her tae see whar I grew up, an tae introduce her tae da fokk in my life. Mam wis insistent at we haed tae bide at dirs, though, an so dere we wir, makkin wir wye nort.

'How did your mum manage to convince your dad to let us stay?' Marnie aksed, stubbin her ciggie oot on da peerie waa afore wis. Be dis point, we wir passin Hay's Dock, whar da museum and archives an Mareel, da isles' cinema an music venue, were at. Hit wid be nae time afore we'd be dockin at Holmsgarth Pier.

'I dinna think I want tae keen,' I gaffed nervously. 'I juist hoop he'll no start ony buddir.'

'That's what I'm afraid of,' Marnie said. 'I know he doesn't like me.'

I jarred whan I heard yun, an hit guid quiet atween wis. You coulda cut da silence laek paet. Finally I said, 'Den yun's his problem. He'll juist hae tae dael wi it. Naebody else minds.'

'It's just we'll be in his house,' shö pointit oot.

'Hit's Mam's hoose as weel,' I assured her. 'Baith dir neems is on da mortgage, shö remindit me o yun. If he starts bein a shit, I promise I'll hae a wird wi him.'

'I'll hold you to that, Lex,' shö said, her eyebroos raised. 'Anyway—we're not letting him spoil the weekend. C'mon, let's get a pic.'

Wi yun, shö pulled me in nixt til her, near anoff at we wir cheek tae cheek, an we smiled as shö pressed da button tae tak da photo o wis. We looked brawly windswept in da feenished product, but Marnie wisna carin. 'Windswept and interesting,' shö grinned, 'and besides, I want everyone on Insta to see how windy it actually is here.'

As shö said yun, Holmsgarth Pier cam intae view, an we guid back inside tae pack up wir cabin. Be da time da gangplank wis secure we wir baith desperate tae win onshore, but Marnie mair so eftir da hellish night shö wis haed. We won doon da stair an dere wis Mam waitin, an shö gae wis baith muckle bosies afore helpin wis oot tae da car wi wir luggage.

Da drive back tae me fokk's hoose wis uneventful—Mam juist engaged wis aboot uni an how it wis goin, an despite da early ooer Marnie seemed brawly happy tae yarn wi her. I couldna really concentrate on dem, though, fir I windered whit Dad wis goin tae say whan we arrived yundir.

He wis thankfully still sleepin whan we got dere, so Marnie an me got intae me room an got unpacked. Marnie lay doon on da bed, an I sat up nixt till her. Shö reached oot an slipped her haand intae mine.

'We got any plans for today?' shö axed, soondin a peerie bit sleepy.

'Hoopfully seein me granny,' I telt her. 'Shö's keen tae meet de, although I doot du mebbe needs a peerie neeb first.'

'A what, sorry?' Marnie gaffed.

I rolled me eyes. 'A *little nap*,' I repeatit in English. Sooth Lexie wis firmly oot o da pictir fir eanoo.

'I'm just joking, chick,' shö said. 'But aye, one of those sounds grand right about now.'

'Fine dat,' I said, an I left her tae it.

Eftir Marnie wis haed her peerie neeb, we got ready tae

set aff tae Granny Gracie's. It turned oot, though, at Dad wis takkin wis an no Mam.

'I hae ower muckle tae dö aroond here,' Mam said, 'but I'm sure shö'll be blyde tae see you baith.'

I wisna worried aboot Granny Gracie. Shö wisna as bad aboot me bein wheer as Dad wis been, which wis a pleasant surprise tae me, but dan shö wis readily acceptit whan een o her cousin's grandsons cam oot a few year afore me. Whan I wis finally telt her, shö wis genuinely delightit, an telt me as lang as I wis happy den shö wis blyde fir me an dat shö wis hoopin I wid bring Marnie hame tae meet her afore lang. Dat bein said, I wisna lookin forwird tae da drive wi Dad.

We sat dere in da car in silence fir maist o it, although Dad haed his phone shipped up tae da car stereo, an hit wis playin Tom Petty and the Heartbreakers' *Greatest Hits* album. Yun wis ay a faimly staple fir wis whan I wis growin up, an he ay lat me pit it on in da car whan he wis drivin me plaesses. I windered if hit wis juist da first thing at cam on whan he startit da car, or if he wis pat it on fir me as some kind o peace offerin.

We arrived at Granny Gracie's an whan we won in da door shö swept me up in her airms an gae me a massive bosie, laek shö ay did, an hit wis fine tae keen nithin wis really cheenged wi her. I introduced her tae Marnie an shö did da sam, which took Marnie be surprise but shö didna seem tae mind ower muckle really. Granny Gracie made wis aa sit doon while shö made tae an got biscuits oot fir wis. Shö wis in her aerly nineties noo, an no mebbe as steady on her feet as afore, but onythin shö could do hersel, shö insistit on.

'Can I give you a hand at all, Mrs Peterson?' Marnie axed.

'Nah, nah, lass,' Granny Gracie insistit, 'I'll be aaright. Set de doon. Oh, an du kin caa me Gracie. Aabody does.' An wi dat shö nippit back intae da keetchin.

'Shö laeks her independence,' I explained as Marnie did whit shö wis telt an sat doon, 'an as du kin see shö doesna hae muckle o yun nooadays.'

'She's adorable,' cooed Marnie. 'You should get her to come down and visit us sometime!'

'Shö's no dat big on flyin or ferries sadly,' I telt her.

'Du kin say yun ageen,' Dad piped up. 'I mind her bein godless feart o da escalators ee time at we wir in Aiberdeen—got her tae geng up een an shö widna come doon ageen!'

'Oh, bless,' Marnie said, tryin no tae gaff, 'that's a wee shame for her. Do you not have any buildings with escalators up here then?'

'Nope,' I said.

'Is that why they're still such a novelty to you when we go out shopping?'

'Yun an double decker buses!'

Granny Gracie cam back in wi da tae an biscuits, an assortment o chocolate eens an sandwich type eens, mainly da sam eens shö wis been buyin aa my mindeen. Eftir shö wis sortit aabody oot, shö cam an sat wi wis, an I saa her tak Marnie's spare haand as shö wis spaekin. I tried tae catch Marnie's een in case shö wis uncomfortable, but shö didna seem tae mind ower muckle.

We spent a lovely efternuin wi Granny Gracie, an whan it cam time fir wis tae geng hame shö gae baith o wis a massive bosie.

'It's been lovely to meet you at last,' Marnie gushed at her. 'Lexie's always telling me loads about you.'

'Hit's been fine tae meet de as weel,' Granny Gracie said. 'I'm been dat keen tae meet de fae de an Lexie started pallin aroond. You pair seem dat blyde o een anidder. Du'll need tae come an see me ageen!'

Pallin aroond—o coorse, yun's no a term shö wid ivver use tae describe da relationship me aulder bridder haed wi his wife, or ony o me cousins wi dir idder halves. It wis anidder wye at I stood oot laek a sair toomb, but apairt fae her choice o wirds me granny wis still acceptit me and wis clearly been chuffed tae meet me girlfreend, so I figured shö could still laern. Besides, shö wis noteeced as weel at we wir happy, which wis mair as Dad wis don.

He mosst o haed a think aboot whit shö wis said tae wis, becis whan we wir on da wye hame, he struck up a conversation wi Marnie.

'Your mum's a total sweetheart,' she said tae him. 'Honestly, she's so cute. I adore her.'

'Maist fokk does,' Dad said, smeegin. I wis startin tae notice a muckle cheenge in him fae yun veesit. Mebbe seein me granny bein lovin an acceptin o me an me girlfreend wis pitten him tae shem somehow, but noo he wis saftenin towards her in a wye I wisna seen yit.

Whan we won hame, Dad parked up da car an we got oot. Dan he said, 'Whan's yun Pride thing you're goin tae? Is it da moarn?'

I jarred a peerie bit hearin him ax, but I said '…yea, da moarn's moarneen.'

'Whit time?' he axed nixt.

'Da parade starts at eleevin,' I telt him, 'but if we want tae be pairt o it we need tae be in Lerook lang afore yun. Dir musterin doon on Commercial Street whar da Royal Bank an da Bookshop is.'

Dad haed a peerie think. Dan he said, 'Could I gie you a lift in?'

Me an Marnie lookit at een anidder, her juist as shocked as me. Dan we lookit at him.

'Weel Mam wis gjaan tae run wis,' I said, 'but I'm sure shö winna mind de offerin.'

'I'm happy tae,' he shrugged. 'Means you'll no need tae be up quite sae early fir da bus. Although we kin geng tae da Harbour Cafe fir sassermaet rolls first if you laek?'

'What's 'sassermaet'?' axed Marnie.

'Hit's basically sausage maet but no in da shape o a sausage,' Dad said. 'Kinda laek yun Lorne gaer at you get doon da rodd, but better.'

'Oh,' said Marnie. 'Aye, that sounds lovely, doesn't it Lexie?'

'Yea, I'm aa fir yun,' I said, smilin at Dad.

'An kin I come an watch you in dis procession?' he axed wis.

'Of coorse,' I telt him.

'Fine dat,' he said, 'we'll geng in fine an aerly an get you pair fed afore you geng mairchin. Hit'll be a fun tae be pairt o, I'm sure.'

He gently tapped baith wir shoodirs in a freendly, weel meanin kind o wye, an as we aa guid back intae da hoose tagidder, I fun mesel tryin no tae greet. I wis been so anxious aboot dis trip, an noo Dad wis cheengin his tune at lang lest. Hit wis juist a peerie gesture eanoo, but hit wis a start, an no only wis it fine tae tinkit me dad wis acceptin me an me girlfreend at last, but noo it wis startin tae at Shetland Lexie could be safely an openly wheer da sam as Sooth Lexie wis.

Alyson Kissner

FLOCCINAUCINIHILIPILIFICATION

After the spelling bee
I forget how to language

or rather I forget how to speak

I speak too much or too little
or say t-o-o-m-u-c-h-a-l-t-o-g-e-t-h-e-r
at the same time

I contradict myself after telling
a story where nothing happens
by repeating *nothing happens*

like an avalanche returns
to the top of its mountain
to gather a particular stone

I describe this glutlack to my therapist
as *holding ten plates with one hand*
or *eating one plate with ten dishes*

because only one meal to one plate
would prove all the ways I am lacking

(it would have been more accurate
to say *your tongues just can't taste it*

like aldehyde in a fist of cilantro
or a dog making love to a bone)

how do I explain all the ways
I was wronged that are right to me

(still knowing they were wrong)

when I use my life in a sentence
I ask for pain with set conditions

floccinaucinihilipilification*

how many letters does it take
to repeat each decision I have made
/will make/keep making

/keep making

*Definition: The action or habit of estimating something as worthless.

Elspeth Wilson

TO THE GIRLS BLASTING AVRIL LAVIGNE WITH THE WINDOWS DOWN

We only spend ten seconds in each others'
company. Me, shoulders drooping, cooling
sweat on my armpits. You, heads thrown
back, streaks of blonde highlights catching
the glow of the streetlights. It's been a week
that's stretched its hands around my neck
from behind, and the only thing I've had
to cling to is a sliver of a moon like the
imprint of a fingernail on skin. And then,
you two. In a small, unflashy car—I will never
know what kind—blasting the chorus
that brings me back to hair swishing, air
guitaring in the laundry cupboard
where parental eyes couldn't find me. To
my first CD, the possibility of 2002, ripped
jeans and hair straightened till it fried.
You still have that energy, that rev, that engine
fire that keeps you singing as you drive away
from me. You obey the speed limit, sound
fading out after the next set of lights.
I don't quite chase you but I speed

up, my heart playing hopscotch, as I
lose you. Your laughter a final gift,
spelling out the sugary depths
of a spring evening with the windows
rolled down in a language I'd forgotten
I still know how to speak.

CONTRIBUTORS

Adi Novak

Adi Novak lives in Glasgow. Their work explores queer bodies and history through poetry and short fiction, and is featured in *Extra Teeth* and *Gutter*. In 2022 they completed an MA in English Literature at the University of Glasgow, where they're currently pursuing an MLitt in Creative Writing.

Alyson Kissner

Alyson Kissner is a winner of the Edwin Morgan Poetry Award and placed second in the 2023 Bridport Poetry Prize. She has also been shortlisted for the Women Poets' Prize and twice shortlisted for the Scottish Book Trust New Writers Award. Her writing can be found at alysonkissner.com or @alykissner

A W Earl

A W Earl is a writer, storyteller and poet whose work is concerned with gender, deviant bodies, and folklore. Their poetry has been published and performed in many venues, including headlining an event at the 2023 Maidstone Fringe. *Time's Fool*, their debut novel was published by Unbound in 2018.

Cal Bannerman

Cal Bannerman is a freelance writer and editor based in Glasgow. Their writing is published in *Extra Teeth, Gutter, Reflex Fiction, Interpreter's House,* and *New Maps*. They served as The Hugo Burge Foundation's Writer-in-Residence 2023, and were Highly Commended for the Bridge Awards x Moniack Mhor Emerging Writer Award 2024.

Carrie Marshall

Carrie Marshall has been a professional writer for 25 years and has written, co-written or ghost-written over 20 non-fiction books. Her memoir about coming out as trans, *Carrie Kills A Man* (404 Ink, 2022), was shortlisted in the Discover category of the 2023 British Book Awards. She lives in Glasgow with her children, a greyhound and too many guitars.

Ciara Maguire

Ciara Maguire is a writer living in Glasgow. Her work has been published in *Extra Teeth, bath magg, SPAM Zine, Gutter, Propel Magazine* and more. Her debut pamphlet, *Impossible Heat*, was published in 2024 with Little Betty Press.

Colin Herd

Colin Herd is a poet and Lecturer in Creative Writing at University of Glasgow. His books include *Too Ok* (2011), *Glovebox* (2013), *Oberwilding—with SJ Fowler* (2015), *Click & Collect* (2017), *Swamp Kiss* (2018), *You Name It* (2019) and *Cocoa & Nothing—with Maria Sledmere* (2023). He was highly commended in the Forward Prizes in 2013 and his work has also been included in the anthology *100 Queer Poems* edited by Andrew McMillan and Mary Jean Chan.

Colin McGuire

Colin McGuire is a Glaswegian living in Edinburgh. In 2018 he published a pamphlet, *Enhanced Fool Disclosure* with Speculative Books. He won the Out-Spoken Prize for Best Poem and Film in 2018 for his poem 'The Glasgae Boys'. In 2020, he received the Ignite Fellowship, from the Scottish Book Trust to work on a new collection of poetry. He facilitates writing workshops as part the Live Literature Program with the Scottish Book Trust and Open Book Charity.

Elspeth Wilson

Elspeth Wilson is a writer interested in exploring the limitations and possibilities of the body. Her poetry pamphlet, *Too Hot to Sleep*, is published by Written Off Publishing. Her debut novel, *These Mortal Bodies*, is forthcoming with Simon and Schuster in 2025. She can usually be found in or near the sea.

Ely Percy

Ely Percy is an award-winning Scottish writer and the author of a memoir *Cracked* (2002) and two novels *Vicky Romeo Plus Joolz* (2019) and *Duck Feet* (2021). Their story 'My Happiness' is a prequel to their novel-in-progress, *Kingstreet*.

Etzali Hernandez

Etzali Hernández is a nonbinary latinx poet, coder, and DJ. Published in various publications, their work includes a poetry pamphlet, *from murky waters, we rise*. They have co-curated projects like *Sore Loser Zine* and *Grief Offerings: (End of) Life Wishes*. Etzali is a member of the Scottish BPOC Writer Network.

Eve Brandon

Eve Brandon (they/them) lives in Glasgow. They work in archives and keep busy writing horrid little stories. Their most recent work has been featured in *CloisterFox* and *The Crow's Quill*. You can find them on Twitter at @EveBrandon_

Fraser Currie

Fraser Currie is a poet and novelist from Glasgow. His writing has featured in publications including *From Glasgow to Saturn, Seedlings, The Passionfruit Review*, and *METAL*. He has an MLitt in Creative Writing from the University of Glasgow.

Hannah Nicholson

Hannah Nicholson is originally from Shetland but now lives in Aberdeen. She holds an MLitt with Distinction in Creative Writing from the University of Aberdeen and in 2021 she won a Scottish Book Trust New Writers Award. She often writes in Shetland dialect, being keen to see its use increase.

Heather Parry

Heather Parry is a writer of fiction and nonfiction. Her debut novel, *Orpheus Builds a Girl,* was shortlisted for the Saltire Fiction Book of the Year award and longlisted for the Polari First Book Prize. She is also the author of a short story collection, *This Is My Body, Given For You,* a short nonfiction book, *Electric Dreams: On Sex Robots and the Failed Promises of Capitalism*, and writes the Substack *general observations on eggs.* Her next novel, *Carrion Crow,* will be released in February 2025.

Jane Flett

Jane Flett is a Scottish writer based in Berlin. Her work has been commissioned for BBC Radio, and featured in the *Best British Poetry* and *Bi+ Lines* anthologies. She is the author of the novel *Freakslaw* (Doubleday).

Lakshmi Ajay

Lakshmi Ajay is a visual artist, writer and social worker in Mental Health and Addictions. She has performed at the Feminist Cabaret at the Edinburgh Radical Book Fair in November 2023, and is currently a writer-in-residence at ECHO, the editorial platform of Take One Action Film Festival. Her art has been exhibited at Blunt Knife Co. and she has completed a Rhubaba writing salon curated by Lola Olufemi. Her work is inspired by her experiences of migration, finding pockets of community along the way and dreaming of abolitionist futures.

Len Lukowski

Len Lukowski is a writer based in Glasgow. His debut pamphlet, *The Bare Thing*, was published in 2022 by Broken Sleep Books. He won the 2018 Wasafiri New Writing Award for life writing. His first poetry collection, *Bodily Fluids*, will be published in 2025.

Mae Diansangu

Mae Diansangu is a queer poet and spoken word artist from Aberdeen. She has performed at literary festivals across Scotland and appeared on BBC Scotland's Big Scottish Book Club and BBC Radio 4's Tongue and Talk. Her series of poems "black lives, heavy truths" is part of the National Library of Scotland's collection. You can read her work in the anthologies *Tales fae the Doric Side* and *Re creation—a queer poetry anthology*. Mae writes in both English and Doric, and her first collection *BLOODSONGS* (Tapsalteerie) was published in Autumn 2024.

Matthew Kinlin

Matthew Kinlin lives and writes in Glasgow. His published works include *Teenage Hallucination* (Orbis Tertius Press, 2021), *Curse Red, Curse Blue, Curse Green* (Sweat Drenched Press, 2021), *The Glass Abattoir* (D.F.L. Lit, 2023) and *Songs of Xanthina* (Broken Sleep Books, 2023).

Niamh Ní Mhaoileoin

Niamh Ní Mhaoileoin is an Irish writer living and working in Edinburgh. Her debut novel, *Ordinary Saints*, will be published in March 2025. As a work-in-progress, it won the PFD Queer Fiction Prize 2022 and was shortlisted for the Women's Prize Discoveries award 2022. Her writing has also appeared in *Gutter, The New Statesman, The Irish Times* and elsewhere.

Paul Brownsey

Paul Brownsey lives in Bearsden. He is a former philosophy lecturer at Glasgow University and a gay rights campaigner from the 1970s. *His book, His Steadfast Love and Other Stories,* was published by Lethe Press. He has a story in *Best British Short Stories 2024* (Salt Publishing).

Pernina Jacobs

Pernina Jacobs is a queer Jewish writer based in Edinburgh. Their work is based around ideas of queerness and community, finding such things in the intersections of identity and small moments of connection. They run community events, including the monthly Wuthering Dykes book club.

Rhys Pearse

Rhys Pearce is a writer and spoken word artist from the Scottish Borders. She was appointed a Young Makar both by Stanza Festival and by the Scottish Poetry Library; and has performed at Dandelion Festival, Wigtown Book Fest, and the Edinburgh Fringe. She is currently working on a debut novel.

River McAskill

River MacAskill is a writer from the north of Scotland based in Glasgow. Notable works include their self-published novel, *Coasting*; the Slow Down per-zine series; the poetry pamphlet *Virility at Home* (Death of Workers Whilst Building Skyscrapers, 2021); and the novella 'A9', in *Hometown Tales: Highlands & Hebrides* (W&N, 2018).

Robbie MacLeoid

Tha Robbie MacLeòid na bhàrd agus sgrìobhaiche, foillsichte ann an iomadach àite, *STEALL* nam measg. Tha e ag obair mar oifigear Gàidhlig. // Robbie MacLeòid's work in various genres has been published by *404 Ink, Gutter, and New Writing Scotland*. He works in Gaelic community organising. He loves the X-Men dearly.

Ross McFarlane

Ross McFarlane is a Glaswegian poet and performer, writing queer stories and small moments with the delivery of a '80s hardcore band. He wrote on horror audio drama series *Folxlore,* winner of Best New Storytelling Production at the 2020 Audio Verse Awards.

Samuel Goldie

Samuel Goldie is a writer focussing primarily on young, queer male experiences in contemporary Scotland. In his spare time he enjoys films, music, running, gymming, pubbing, scranning and *A Song of Ice and Fire.*

Shane Strachan

Shane Strachan's latest book is *DWAMS* (Tapsalteerie). He won Scots Champion at the 2023 Scots Language Awards following his year as the National Library of Scotland's Scots Scriever. Throughout this residency, he explored Anna Gordon Brown's Northeast ballad manuscripts, which partly inspired his Aberdeenshire-set autofiction, 'Bastart Bairn'.

Shola Von Reinhold

Shola von Reinhold is a writer and artist. Her debut novel *LOTE* won the Republic of Consciousness Prize and the James Tait Black Memorial Prize.

Shona Floate

Shona Floate is a Glasgow-based writer from Broughty Ferry, Dundee. Her writing is informed by her own experiences of queer womanhood and family, aiming to dissect the queerness of certain relationalities, especially motherhood and intense female friendships. She completed an MLitt in Women, Writing and Gender at the University of St. Andrews in 2022 and an undergraduate degree in English Literature at The University of Glasgow in 2021.

Suki Hollywood

Born in Belfast on Valentine's Day, Suki Hollywood is a writer and poet. Her self-published debut novel *Jesus Freaks*—a queer thriller—is available now. Her work has been featured in *Gutter, Deleuzine, SPAM, Water Wings* and more. Suki's two poetry pamphlets, *Heart Eyes* and *This Suit,* are available now via www.sukihollywood.com, along with *This Suit*'s companion film, which was included in the SQIFF 2021 selection. In 2023, Suki provided the words for *Yes, I can see the stars*, a billboard campaign for beloved queer venue, Bonjour (RIP).

Titilayo Farukuoye

Titilayo Farukuoye (they/them) is a writer, educator and organiser based in Glasgow. Their work addresses social justice and community care and is informed by dreaming and the radical imagination. Titilayo co-directs the Scottish BPOC Writers Network and is a winner of the 2022 Edwin Morgan Poetry Award. Their debut poetry pamphlet *In Wolf's Skin* is available with Stewed Rhubarb Press.